Twin Oaks

Melissa Palmer

On the outskirts of every agony sits some observant fellow who points.
　　　　　　　　　　　—Virginia Woolf.

CONTENTS

MRS. MACMILLAN'S GARDEN

The entrance to Twin Oaks was guarded by two voiceless giants. They flanked its wrought iron gates with an air of certain permanence even though the neighborhood smelled of fresh paint and newly laid sod. And despite the hint of belonging that clung to the summer breeze, they acted more like outsiders, forbidden lovers ousted from the circle within, branches stretched from either side of the street with yearning fingertips that would never touch.

Mrs. MacMillan loved those trees. They served as dutiful reminders every time she returned home that someone would be there waiting, even if it was just a pair of deciduous sentries. Trips to the big warehouse had become more frequent now that the warm weather had kicked in; but they were necessary, especially here in Twin Oaks.

She turned into the entryway and immediately felt her hands relax. The little hamlet had all the shape and good luck of a horseshoe turned on its side, and she settled knowing that she was back where she was meant to be. One turn removed her from the harshness of the world she briefly visited for basic needs: a jug of milk, a can of coffee, and three bags of diatomaceous earth. Hers was a world of thick emerald greenery and lush, delicious smells, a tiny universe where doors were left open and no one cared that there were no fences to block the view into a neighbor's yard.

Her home, the Grandview, was the largest in the entire subdivision, visible even from outside the gates and standing at the head of what looked like a giant beetle. Hers was the flagship, the masterpiece, mirrored by none but the plantations of old, wrapped in an old-fashioned lemonade-drinking porch, with rocking chairs and oversized hanging plants bursting from their pots. It was a vision in white: two large picture windows on the second floor set off in ebony panels, lacquered to match the double door that marked the entryway. It was simple in its elegance, like Mrs. MacMillan herself.

Three years ago the homeowner's association, then a burgeoning group of well-doers, had honored her for the second year in a row for the assorted flowers that grew in her backyard garden. And she had worn that blue ribbon with honor, nodding humbly at the well-wishers who whispered about the scarlet beauties that graced the small Shangri-La she engineered off the back porch, the bravest of which who asked to sit there amongst the wonders that defied the laws of nature.

She pulled her packages out of the car and waved absently to the youngish mom of two from down the street who ran up and out of the neighborhood at least twice a week. She didn't know her name but admired her begonias and taste in social etiquette. She was not part of the association that insulted and ignored. She was also new enough to the neighborhood to avoid silent judgment and whispered critiques. She didn't look as she passed in front of the empty space that used to be Mrs. MacMillan's garden, not once for what she was too new to remember, and not twice for a wonder she couldn't forget.

Mrs. Granger would be having tea by now. The faint

scent of cinnamon toast came wafting from the house to the right. It was the Victorian Hempstead, not as large as Mrs. MacMillan's but a handsome home, ornately detailed with a nod to the craftsmanship of times gone by, an ode to the decade in which the woman was born. She had no idea how old Mrs. Granger was, a woman of diction and stature whose first name remained unknown. She carried herself with grace, with the air of someone worthy. But her wizened face and paper hands betrayed her to all witnesses. Her house did not show the same wear as her body or disappearing lips, her teeth that seemed unnaturally long, or the slight hump she tried to hide under designer suits. She spoke with the subtle confidence of one who knew she would be queen someday, and the patience of a lady who could wait forever if she had to for her ascent to the crown.

Smiling into Mrs. MacMillan's yard, she'd said, "Perhaps this will be your year..." Accented syllables through the whitewashed planks behind her shriveled lips. Which had sent the younger woman out the first time for three bags of a mix that was certified organic followed by a morning spent tilling the soil. There were no gardeners or husband for Mrs. MacMillan: it was just her, the house and the soft earth.

The Pollacks, to the left, didn't say much. They grilled hamburgers and hot dogs, ate quietly and wrangled their two catalog children back into their Gabled Homestead, a newer and smaller model on the lot that made up for what it lacked in space with high tech construction. Much like the Pollack family, the Gabled Homestead lacked panache and held little interest for Mrs. MacMillan.

She washed the sticky, fetid mess from her hands before her second trip to Mega-mart, this time for lye and a roll of thick plastic to deal with pests that might interfere with her plans. She would cover every angle, account for every variable. As her neighbor had said, this would be her year.

She was patting down the dark patch just in front the bench when the young couple from the far end of the U had walked past again, a ritual the newlyweds shared, looping up and down the curl of their new neighborhood in an attempt to master their new surroundings. They were getting used to things, to each other. Their measured steps matched in rhythm and their pace was punctuated by inward turns and hopeful glances, the kind of hope that only comes with youth and love still fresh. They lived in the Newstead, a relatively tiny model, relegated to the outermost stretch of the Twin Oaks circle. But they kept their lawn manicured and their paint neat. Even the smallest house in the circle was fit to sit on the cover of a greeting card. They made a handsome picture together, and from the look of their house, they were a lot like the walk they took, headed in the right direction.

She looked up to give them a courteous wave and they returned the pleasantry, although their faces looked quizzical. By now they had walked through the neighborhood enough times to have heard the condemnations of the homeowner's association. Still, they wondered why there were no shrubs or tomatoes, but mostly they demanded, in that one unguarded glance, a view of something spectacular, the likes of which they would not forget. Apparently, they were disappointed in her inability to deliver.

That's when the last trip had become so necessary. A touch of diatomaceous earth here and there would bring life where she needed it most.

Her back and hands ached. There were streaks of white on her dark culottes and smears of blackish-brown on her pale skin. Leaves and twigs stuck out from her grayish-white bun that now sat sidesaddle and loose on her head. She was a camouflaged warrior, a strategic solider with an ache inside that rumbled from within.

By the time she finished it was almost time for a late dinner, the sun now losing itself beyond the horizon, only a slight glimmer of blush left on the fat cheek of the sky. Mrs. Womack was out with her genius dog for one last lap around the neighborhood. She held a wad of plastic bags in the free hand she used to wave. How the woman could look so perpetually confused was beyond Mrs. MacMillan. At heart she didn't care enough to give it more thought. She had bigger things on which she needed to focus every shred of concentration.

She wasn't interested in television or music. The day had sucked her dry. As soon as her dinner settled she was curled up in bed, resting, planning for tomorrow morning. But each time her mind faded into the blackness of sleep, and each time that a small blossom of color pushed its way up through her semi-consciousness, she was interrupted. It wasn't by the splashing of the Pollack children swimming into the late hours of evening. And it wasn't the genius dog howling at an unknown emissary. It was something else, throbbing in her head, a pulse that pulled her toward consciousness and finally from her bed. She left the blankets slack, not bothering to smooth them out before taking leave, an act that would normally weigh on her heavily like an old secret. But *this* was too important...

Under a cloudless sky the woman began to dig. On her hands and knees without the aid of a shovel or spade she sunk her fingers into the moist dark earth and pulled away at the smooth surface so long without blemish or growth. It came up in clumps that sailed through the air. Others settled on her back like sweets on a coffee table. It was cool in the moonlight but her nightgown began to stick and clutch where it hung in the mixture of damp earth and sweat. There was no noise she could hear, only the throbbing that had awoken her from sleep and the labored sounds of her own breath as she dug in and dug deeper using hands and elbows, feet and knees. She pushed with her arms in small circles expelling handfuls of ground, disrupting nothing in the night but a few earthworm homes. She was swimming in it now, silent and determined.

The evening had gone from pitch to gray when she disappeared down into the hole. It was late enough for birds to just begin singing but not early enough for the paperboy to come wheeling by with his news. Neither the birds nor the paperboy heard the sharp sound of nails worked to bone. No one got to see how her face lit up when she knew she had finished and emerged with what she'd found.

They were brilliant in the moonlight, exactly as she'd remembered. She'd extracted them from deep in the earth where they'd been waiting, placed there more out of fear than necessity, the looming threat of critters and prying little hands guiding her every move. The first was in perfect condition, so round and defined, still white and firm to the touch. Some were long and slender, slightly worn and yellowed with time. They looked as though they might fall apart, but all were intact as she'd secretly hoped. Held in the pockets there where she'd dug was the promise of a life the yard had not seen.

When she woke it was later than she'd slept in years but she'd earned that rest with what she'd done. So much of her had gone into the prospect of this very second. She had pulled off the antique lace nightgown for something more suitable and preened for a second or two longer than usual. She wanted to be fresh. She bounded downstairs with youthful steps that challenged her age. Her footfalls were tentative leaving the house, a child's tiptoe to the Christmas tree. Though it was late, the dew was still sticking to blades of grass in tiny diamond dots that tickled her ankles and cooled the pads of her feet as she entered the yard. The day was warmer than expected but this was not surprising. It was the scent that was unmistakably new. Mrs. MacMillan's breath caught in her throat, swept away by the fragrant smell of summer luscious roses and honey dipped blossoms, fat with dew. Their ripe petals were open and rose to the air awaiting the sun's kiss. They grew tall and full climbing the sides of the bench, underneath it, around it in bright paralyzing blues and electrifying oranges, deep dark fuchsias and magenta dotted with tiny buds of purple, flowers she didn't remember planting, blooms she'd never seen before. And the smell, it was too much to take in.

But in the center of it all was her gem, the treasure for which she'd toiled without the help of a gardener or son; no other set of hands was there to help her extricate the marvel that would surely bring the association to her door. Amid the bright white Calla Lily, plump and flirtatious, the miraculous rainbow that burst around the bench like a Technicolor frame comprised solely of fireworks, sat the wonder that made everything so.

It was almost difficult to make it out, the flora overtaking the bench like ants on a dropped candy, so that it lost the stone look completely, instead becoming a plush, multicolored sofa bursting with light, interrupted only at its center where the figure rested. Two pockets sat in a canvas of dazzling white, only now instead of dark and emptiness they were overflowing with turquoise sweet peas. A hat sat slightly askew atop the shiny globe that had maintained its bleached white complexion among the tendrils of cosmos and thick leafy green, a discovery that took Mrs. MacMillan's heart soaring. There were no whitewashed planks, only two neat rows of ivory smiling on the accomplishment, on the good morning. One slender hand was raised as if to say so.

His suit looked so good. The whole neighborhood looked good.

Bees buzzed, birds chirped and the sweet smell of her garden drowned out Mrs. Granger's midmorning tea.

From here the woman could see all the way out of Twin Oaks. She could see the cars approaching all the way from the road, her favorite trees outside the gates looking in, and her own neighbors as they approached her proud site. Some came on foot, pointing and staring. There were children on bicycles, perhaps the Pollack's children or of the lady who ran. Others drove slowly from further down the U.

Mrs. MacMillan stood in front of the thick luxurious blooms and the treasure she unearthed, waving exuberantly to anyone and everyone who came past.

Mrs. Womack came closest with her genius retriever. She stood with her mouth hanging wide just as the dog. They both took in the wonder, finally looking as if they understood.

GUSTAV'S LEASH

The sun shone against a veil of blue silk, its only companion the lone Buddha grinning down on a day that felt much more like spring than July. Mrs. Womack didn't mind the early hour or the fact that Gustav, ever a creature of habit, had grown quite entitled to the daily jaunt. There was something in his pleading eyes each time that she could not resist, like he knew a secret he couldn't share. Those eyes were deep pools, and she could never quite see the bottom, though that did not stop her from trying. It was that will to try that found her outside well before the coffee was brewed.

The day was fresh, and Twin Oaks had a life all its own with none of the trappings of a neighborhood wide-awake. All the moms and dads and SUVs and big wheels were still sound-asleep, tucked far away from the parkway in the safety of a garage. The inner circle belonged to the crickets that sang their morning praise to the squirrel that shook her tail in Samba, perhaps seducing the rabbit who stood frozen pretending not to be seen. Bumbles and birds flew overhead in an airborne ballet, making ribbons in the sky and avoiding the more common fast and frantic straight line that only occurs when fleeing. Despite the woman's feigned protests, it was her favorite time of day, long before the droning importance of numbers overtook the sound of the true worker bees.

"Well aren't you just the dapper Dan this morning, Gustav?" He had stopped on the second step to take a quick sniff of his surroundings. "You know, you look like a movie star when you stand like that."

He sauntered off the landing without blush. He was used to compliments from his longtime companion, and within a few panted breaths they had retreated into the silence that accompanies comfort, relying on what was around them, their own steps joining the symphony.

"I like the way your hair falls over your eye. That new shampoo suits you, you know. I don't know if it's these flowers but I smell something sweet, and I think it's you." Her breath caught in the back of her throat, not from shock or sadness or even an accidentally inhaled bit of saliva. Air didn't come as easily as the donuts and pies seemed to lately. She was reminded of that every day, though these little walks together helped her to forget.

He lowered his head as if fascinated by his own armpit.

"Oh, don't be like that, silly. You're as sweet as the day is long. There's no need to be bashful." She gave his shoulder a pat and ruffled his shiny golden hair.

They padded along a stretch bathed in sunlight and birdsong. But when he stopped she was grateful. He was the younger and more fit of the two, and he could hear her breaths as they became shallow and syncopated. They paused in silence in front of a large white house with an ebony door, dead center in the Twin Oaks loop, while she fished a tissue out of her shorts pocket and patted at her glossy cheek.

"You're awfully quiet, honey. Don't you like the new hedge? It's had to have grown a full half an inch since it went in. And it's only been a week. Must be some great soil. Makes a world of difference, you know, not seeing straight back into that yard any longer. Wouldn't you say?"

As usual, he didn't. But nonetheless she pressed on with a smile on her face and as much bounce in her step as her less than graceful body would allow.

The coffeepot was full and steaming by the time they arrived home. Mr. Womack stood completely hidden behind the open refrigerator door.

"Oh good, you're having breakfast with us," she beamed. But no sooner had the words come out of her mouth, than the back of his head was disappearing through the kitchen entryway. From the backhanded wave she could make out the silhouette of a lone banana already bitten. "All right then, I was just going to fix something for me and for Gustav. You'd like some eggs, right honey? They're good for your hair." She called back through the door to the phantom that was eating the banana. "If you change your mind, there will be some toast too. I'll make whole wheat if you like."

He was working again, always working. Despite tax season being long over he'd been at it on some accounting company's finances or investments. Algorithms, she thought he'd said. He could have said pie À la mode for all she knew or cared. Math was completely beyond her, even in the smallest form, never mind that computer.

She should have been used to this by now; the years of his imprisonment locked away in the confines of that paper mountain he called his office. He was hooked up to that computer like it was a life support machine, but why would she question that? That's how he'd met her, after all.

By the time she'd cleared the dishes a thick orange yolk hung overhead; the day was rich and full of promises that she did not want to miss. They pushed out barely saying good-bye to the man who worked the keys in the back room with the locked door.

"Oh honey, you look like a hero when you stand like

that."

Gustav paused on the second step, this time taking in the scents of cut grass and sweaty bodies. The sun caught in his golden hair just as the breeze lifted unseasonably, framing him in the halo that Mrs. Womack knew was always there. That very same breeze saved her in an instant from the stifling heat she'd felt inside.

"Oh look! It's Mollie and Alton and that munchkin of theirs. Hello, dears!"

She waved at the sister and brother coated in a thin layer of dust and summer stickiness. Toddling close behind was the one in green carrying a lollipop much too large for his little hand.

"Hello, Pigg. My, how big you're getting! You know, I bet you've grown a full inch since I saw you last. You're almost as big as your brother now."

Everyone but Pigg was aware of the lie but smiled as the little one grinned wide, standing tall and straight and looking like a tow-headed string bean.

"Ima rockit asher knot," the child said proudly.

"Gustav says you'll make a fine astronaut, Piggy." She winked at the older children.

Alton, the eldest and most cynical of the three, gaped at Gustav and then at the woman. "No one ever understands Pigg."

The woman nodded at her friend with a response that she'd given just about everyone in the neighborhood.

"Gustav is really smart."

With a wink and a pat the duo was off, leaving the children to do as they would on such a glorious and refreshing day, but she waited a few ticks before addressing her companion's quizzical backward glance.

"Well, I don't know either Gustav, it's hard to tell." He leaned against her leg as they walked as a single creature. "Yes, you are right about that. Some pink or blue would help. No, Gustav, I don't know why they don't tell anyone. That is their business to know, not ours."

She stopped short and framed his face with her hands, looking him right in the eyes. "I don't *know* what kind of name that is, actually, but I won't make any further comment. Who am I to judge anyone?" She gave him an affectionate ruffle as they moved on.

"What do you suppose people would say about a person who marries someone they met on an Internet dating site? The comments would not be entirely positive, you can bet on that."

He paused again, this time lifting his nose.

"I smell it too, dear. It must be tea-time for Mrs. Granger."

The stately home with the pink door favored their senses once a day with an airy cinnamon cloud. The woman inside was just as stately. Mrs. Womack often admired her silky suits and fancy jackets, the way her white hair looked ice-cold in the heat and at the same time resistant to unpredictable summer breezes. She was graceful and light on her feet, though she stood tall and confident, like a Prime Minister or Head of State. And she knew the importance of a snack around midday.

She grabbed three croissants from the kitchen pantry, stuffing one with ham and cheese, smearing the other with a bit of lemon curd and honey. But the fate of the third hung in the air in her frozen hand. "Oh, don't crinkle your nose like that. It's the same stuff I put in the pies. Where's your sense of adventure?"

Gustav wasn't sold on the yellow contents of the glass jar open on the table. He sniffed at it cautiously, and with a lick thought the better of the sour spread.

"It's not for everyone. Don't be hard on yourself. At least you tried."

She smeared the last croissant with a bit of cream cheese and peanut butter and served it to him as dessert, after chicken hearts and beef.

The house was dark and hot, shut up like an attic box, curtains drawn tight against the day and holding out sunlight and air. Her skin felt like bubbling dough in a wood fire oven, uncomfortable and itchy, and her throat had the constricted feeling of allergic reactions or walking through smoke.

Mr. Womack emerged from his office for a refill of coffee and a few sesame seed breadsticks. He wasn't interested in the lady's wares, not even a sniff. He turned around returning to the office before she could ask why he kept the television tuned to the channel with ant fights, and why he kept the volume so high, and why he'd turned off the air conditioning but hadn't opened the windows. She waddled down the hallway looking for answers, and more paper towels from the hall closet, and as she padded the pool on her neck she heard him from the other side of the door.

"I can hear you breathing out there, for God's sake. You know, I can think of at least two reasons you're always so hot."

She turned back toward the closet to grab another roll for good measure, buffering the sounds of his suggestions with absorbent relief. She made sure her breathing was calm and even when she approached again to make amends, but he was already talking to his colleague online. She could hear the voice coming through loud and clear, replacing the static she'd heard earlier, PersianPrince_15. He seemed to help him out a lot lately, for hours at a time, even late into the night.

The only reprieve from the hot stale air that seemed to plume from the walls flooded her in citrus-scented bubbles as she scrubbed in the sink. She kept the water cool and let it flow over her forearms and elbows, humming to herself as she assessed the day laid before her. Mr. Womack hadn't emerged for an early supper. Even when she'd called to him it had seemed that the static coming from his computer commanded his attention. "Do you want some supper? DO YOU WANT SOME SUPPER? Hello?"

He didn't even bother to open the door but shouted

through it, which was as disappointing as his absence. The heat was strongest in this part of the house. She imagined the quick rush of air that would come when he opened the door but instead heard the muffled shout.

"No. I don't want supper. I don't need to eat all thetime."

Her voice wilted, melting inward as she swallowed under a practiced yet determined smile. "Doesn't all that static drive you crazy? You can't hear anything."

There was no pause, only the quick answer that was followed by footsteps and the return of that irritating sound.

"No, no it doesn't."

Between a second helping of soapy water and creeping back to the door, time got the better of her. The sun ducked under the horizon, a sliver of pink grapefruit dipping onto colored sugar.

"It is beautiful Gussie, isn't it?"

He looked like a commandant on an old time ship taking in the light blue sky that was the forbearer of good things to come.

"We'll miss it if we stand around like statues!"

And with that he snapped to. It was late enough in the afternoon that at any other time of year it would have been called evening. Had it been winter, the Pollack children would already be in their baths or winding down for dreams of milky skies and intergalactic travels. In the twilight they were still going strong, playing big wheels among the lightning bugs. This was Mrs. Womack's second favorite time of day, the time when the day creatures ceded their domain to the true nocturnes, the owls and bats. Somehow, when the night was black, something ominous took over. Even the beloved circle of Twin Oaks looked more sinister when draped in the shadows of things unseen. When mystery hung in the air, Mrs. Womack preferred to stay inside.

"Let's go, little man. We don't want to miss the show!"

They looked comical together, Gustav smooth and graceful cutting through the air like an oiled blade, and Mrs. Womack, pallid and encumbered by her own limbs. She was beyond embarrassment. She gave all that up the day of her wedding as she stood lopsided next to her tiny new mate who never once returned her gaze. She leaned like a swollen Pisa, wrapped in lace, in the only photo they had, her smile not yet as practiced but just as determined. Her rubber shoes squeaked under a combination of pressure and sweat. Yet she pushed on despite an ever-so-light headwind until they reached the house with the pink door. If she waited for the breeze to calm, she could make out the faint hiss and scratch of needle finding groove. And in that, it was worth it all, all the wayward hairs clinging to her face, the faint burning in her chest as her wind returned. To most it was undetectable, a hint of cinnamon that hung in the air like a friendly neighborhood ghost. Things like that were underscores that most people didn't see. But Mrs. Womack lived for those lines.

"I never would have pegged her for Ragtime, Gussie, but isn't it lovely?"

She imagined Mrs. Granger performing a soft-shoe inside, perhaps leafing through old scrapbooks filled with pictures of Vaudevillians and Burlesque queens. She couldn't help but sway to the music as she and her companion slowed their walk so not to miss a measure of the song. It wouldn't come again until tomorrow at this same time.

And as if an invisible hand cranked at the woman's back, she sped up past the large house with the black door and hedge, the one that elicited no sound, then slowed again approaching the little ones on their "big rigs" who disappeared down the driveway and into the backyard. For that Mrs. Womack felt lucky. It wasn't that she didn't want to see them, but at this time of day she was more interested in what she might hear.

The children's father would disappear after dinner into

the garage from where the most curious sounds would erupt. Sometimes it was great banging, or splashing water; other times silence followed by gasping breaths.

"Do you think that hurts, Gussie? That earring he's got up top? And that beard of his has grown at least an inch since I last saw him. Don't look at me like that. You remember. During that Memorial Day thing when they were showing off the new houses. He was wearing a white t-shirt."

He was giving something up; she had seen it that day, maybe coffee. He fidgeted as if trying not to scratch at an itch that he couldn't relieve. Sometimes, when he turned a certain way, she could see something colorful peeking out of the sleeve; sometimes it bled through the white. At first she was worried he might be cut, the way he pawed at it, but then realized his secret. She had tried not to stare, but whatever it was, it was large and colorful and must have covered his entire upper arm.

She smiled feeling her face grow pink where the apples pushed up under her eyes.

Mr. Pollack didn't care what other people thought of him.

She wondered if he was doing Bohemian things back there, the likes of which bearded folks with earrings would surely do in the middle of the summer.

"Sounds like Mr. Chalmers is at it too..."

The mournful song of a Spanish guitar had crept across the circle as they ventured further into the last walk of the day. This last hook made her love Twin Oaks all the more. With a single loop she was whisked to the faraway places of which she only dreamed. And she was able to do things she would never do, all in broad daylight with no risk of hurt or torment or judgment. She walked a few steps and was a street performer, or a ballerina, or in her most secret places, a can-can girl at the Moulin Rouge.

"Mrs. Womack, right?"

She was ducked down paying Gustav a service of true

companionship but didn't need to look up. She recognized the voice. With a warm and freshly-tied baggy in her dominant hand she jolted upright in a motion that made her wobbly. But none of that mattered because he already had her left hand in his, lifting her to unshakable ground.

She looked deep into two dark eyes that seemed to devour the surroundings like tiny black holes. She dived down into them hoping to drown. They darted now and then to Gussie, then to the baggie and to her moistly soiled knee, but she held on following their dance.

"Wilma. Call me Wilma."

Her breath was strong and she was thankful for not sounding wheezy or weak. And she found herself standing straight and tall, somehow more familiar with her surroundings.

"Well, it's nice to meet you in person, Wilma. I hear that Gustav here is very smart." He gave him a pat on the head and her companion responded just as Wilma did, straightening out his back, standing taller than usual.

She felt her face erupt in spontaneous sunshine as she grabbed her golden friend in a well-deserved hug and couldn't surmise whether or not she'd said thank you, or good-bye, or anything for that matter, before she'd turned to go on her way.

"I'm Jack, by the way," he had called to her, this time rubbing his long whiskers. "Not Jackson, that is, just Jack."

"All right then. Just Jack," she said over her shoulder while smiling in a way that she hadn't smiled in years.

"Good night, Wilma," he said and waved, his other hand drifting to the phantom itch.

It was so hard to breathe in this house.

She pulled the note like Excalibur from a bowl of grapes on the kitchen table where it sat in wait for her return. It said things like *necessity* and *hiding* and a whole bunch of other words that came in hiccups as she read through the page. The static was blaring from the back room. He'd no doubt departed in a hurry after planting his notice in her beautiful fruit.

Without knowing why she walked toward the room to which she was never granted entrance and tried the knob. It was open, of course, but what was shocking was that he was still there. His back was to the door that he'd absently left unlocked, and he was so taken with his own rushed words that he didn't notice her or the fact that she'd gone out and come back holding a thick loop of leather in her hands. He was too busy speaking non-business words to the one who was neither Persian nor prince, the one who looked agape onscreen watching Wilma Womack creep in from behind.

"I got back faster than I thought I would." Her voice was smooth and confident despite the heat that radiated from the walls.

The thin man sat helpless beneath her heavy hand as she dangled Gustav's leash just in front of his slender throat. Before he could offer a word she was upon him, close to his face and speaking into his ear. It was closer than they'd been during their entire courtship.

"You will be gone before I return."

She wasn't asking.

She turned on her heel with grace and dignity, walking tall. She didn't look back and called over her shoulder. "And open the windows before you go!"

She and Gustav moved with a singular mind, without pause or hesitation. They walked directly, a silken ribbon, a pas de deux in motion and certainty as they pushed past the threshold and straight into the darkness.

MR. POLLACK IN THE EYES OF A MADWOMAN

*E*verything about her was perfect. Yet there was that weird empty feeling, like reaching into a pocket he swore was full only to come up with a hand full of lint. It gnawed at him inside, as if he'd left something undone, an appliance he'd left running, something burning on the stove. It was hard to live that way, looking over his shoulder for phantoms that weren't there. It made him itch. And it was something he could never make her understand. Jack felt guilty for it every morning when he disappeared into the shed, every time he looked at her, every second he hid behind a bush debating whether or not to light the match.

She was still in bed. She would sleep for the better half of the morning, serene as a seamless doll. He could be sure of it today. Last night the Chardonnay flowed fast and steady, as it always did after a big closing. Soon the Harbages would be settled into the neighborhood, and that would officially cross the most difficult-to-push home off of her list. It was just last week that they were mere renters. But she'd convinced them, newlyweds or not, to take the plunge. The enormity of this feat in her eyes was hard to fathom, but she had persisted as always, and succeeded in her effort to complete this circle, her personal heaven: Twin Oaks.

He ducked into a shadow as the sun peeked over the horizon.

The shed was tucked beneath two crepe myrtles. He was thankful for the curtain they dropped in front of the door. They provided precisely enough cover to save the one spot of the Homestead he could call his own. It was a blot on the landscape, she said, but as long as it couldn't be seen from the street she had let it slide. It wasn't much to look at, a relic from times gone by, possibly put there by the construction staff when the foundation was being poured, a tiny sore thumb that stuck out forty yards from the palace. But he liked it for all that it was. He appreciated the wear-worn shingles and the way it leaned like a drunk refusing to lie down and sleep it off.

Of all the things he might be doing right now, was smoking really that bad? It didn't bloat his liver or make him mean. It didn't make him go digging for a fight. Hell, it was nothing like—he didn't want to think about all the things it wasn't like.

But she didn't see it that way. If she saw him standing here, match in hand, it would be war. Of that he was sure. It was the smell, she said, that she hated most. It lingered on his clothes and smudged the furniture with marks that no one but her could see. She had an eye for imperfection. She could root it out from a mile away. She could sniff out lost revenue from two towns over, and God forbid they lose a cent. The price of their home meant something much different to her than to him. She talked about the house's cost daily, as if she would ever part from her bastion. He knew the objection had less to do with resale and more to do with regard. Her fellow homeowners would never condone that scent in the house, let alone keeping company with the likes of people who did. She couldn't abide by such heinous disregard for property value. And so she made the decision to disapprove just as she made most others—by association.

In this light the house gleamed like polished stone, more so than any other on the block. Mrs. Granger gushed over the care she'd taken to plant Double Flowering Almond along the periphery of the property. Crass, she said, were the neighbors who settled for lazy landscaping, simple hedges and apple trees. They were amateurs who didn't know better, she said. But the high maintenance choice exemplified personal care. The blooms screamed it from their delicate stems.

He didn't care either way. But April almost burst like a balloon when she received such a compliment from the matriarch of the clan. Meanwhile, it had been he who had picked the dumb bushes, not because it was the classy decision, but because that's where she was standing at the time when he stopped to talk to her, that lady from down the street, the woman from the big white house, the one they clucked their teeth over—Mrs. MacMillan. He rarely talked to the neighbors in Twin Oaks, at least the ones who showed up for the meetings. But this one was different. She was the one with the roses.

They were legendary, the biddies all said over clinking glasses, but not so for years. He wouldn't know. It was all lost long before he and April had moved in.

She was at the Meg-O-Mart that Sunday he'd skimmed the aisles for items that made no difference at all. But as he gravitated toward the greenhouse he couldn't help but stop at the sight. She stood among the potted plants and fertilizer, hovering over flowerbeds like a ghost. She didn't care that he was looking, or didn't notice. He wasn't sure if she was chanting or praying. An uninformed witness might assume she was merely talking to herself, but they, like so many others, would be mistaken. This was the look of reverent abandon. Whomever it was she addressed was not of this world. Least of all, were they standing in the garden center.

What a strange sight this woman was! Her long braid frayed at the top and bottom, like a school girl on a playground aged decades before she was ready. Light splotches and clods of dirt played war on her denim overalls in a collage of black and blue. She was somewhere that transcended fertilizers and shrubbery, the world of Chardonnay. There was a white smudge under her eye that she didn't notice despite the pink halo of angry skin budding up around it. He dropped the sacks at his sides. And then he did something he could not reason or defend.

He reached for her and brought her hands to him, pulling the woman nearer. It was as if he were taking the limbs of a rag doll. But he wanted to know what it was she'd muttered. He needed those words as much as she did, a gentle lullaby that made him forget himself for one soft second.

It was one of those things a person might experience once in a decade. If they are lucky. He knew what he wanted and what he needed, neither of which were anywhere close to the azaleas and potting soil. The thought overwhelmed him as it mingled with the hushed sounds of the tiny specter in front of him. It buzzed in his ears like electricity. It filled him like promise.

He snatched up the two small trees that flanked Mrs. MacMillan and got out of the store as fast as he could. He left her there to the vigil, grateful for the words she'd shared.

No one seemed interested in this story. Last night, when he finally spoke of that day, they were all more intrigued by the subject of his tale, the one they had condemned. He was the last to see her before the incident. Did she say what she was going to do? What of the mysterious flowers? The words flitted in careless questions so quickly that they melted into a hum he could ignore.

What was she thinking when she dug up that front lawn? They barraged him with hypotheses, all of which had no bearing, thoughts that were as restricted as the ties that bound them all together over hedge heights and ice cream socials. It was beyond their comprehension that the large white house still sat empty. The threat of panic loomed only once with discussions of the lawn. Who'd be tending it now that the old woman was away? The grass had no accountability for its actions and is it edged slowly past ankle high; they looked more and more urgently for someone upon which they could place the blame. They prattled on as if the words he spoke meant nothing, and all the while April stared at him with that look, that compound look of contempt and pity. It told him she stayed despite the differences, because she was stuck now with an investment she could never predict would go bad. But he would never measure up.

The grass was damp this morning, and as he crept out of the shadow he felt each blade just above his foot where the flesh and bone were one.

She'd be sick if she saw him out here, stooping into his shed. If she knew what was in his pocket, or what he was doing all these mornings instead of painting flowerpots like he said he'd do. He unrolled the thick paper and smoothed it under his hands. It was cool, cream-white like an old bone. When he told her he'd bought new linens, he hadn't lied. It was a stretch, but it wasn't a lie. He wouldn't lie.

But the eyes would always betray him.

He had just enough time to lay things out as planned, gentle brushstrokes melting into measure, circles and shadows, lines and light, no questions, merely motion.

The old woman's eyes had drawn him in and kept him there, mesmerized. Her words and being brought him in, but it was her eyes that became the magnet. He couldn't move. They were like cornflowers, not the dead eyes of lost hope, but the kind that dance in the light. His moves were fluid despite the rushed nature of his task. He was precise when he needed to be, laying in the muted tones and trying over to capture that light. He knew those eyes. He would make them his. He gave them life as he painted.

Pigg would be waking up soon. The little one took after him, rising early. The others were more like their mother and would take their time, but the youngest liked the morning sun. He wiped his hands clean of the light blues and golds that colored his nails, and satisfied with what he had done, set back as if the interlude hadn't happened.

The neighborhood was most alive in the morning. The houses looked so much better without the clutter of small talk and posture. If they would have asked him last night, which they hadn't, he would have said that the MacMillan house looked the best it had ever looked now that it stood empty at the head of the Twin Oaks circle. With its stark white face and big dark windows it looked like an old man staring out at all the smaller houses. He knew better than to get involved with all the yard party nonsense and potluck dinners. He was wise in his choice to remain removed from the inner trappings of the lawns committee.

The birds were singing a gentle reminder to pick up the newspaper—it was *trashy* to leave it past the morning, or so he was told, but he was sure that far worse peccadillos were possible. The crickets chirped in agreement. Soon they'd be joined by the footsteps of the lady that ran, the one with the strong arms and the faraway stare. For the most part she kept to herself. But where was she this morning?

He peeled the wrapper from his news before he even brought it in, depositing it in the small silver can marked 'PLASTIC' in the fenced-in nook by the side door. Neglecting such a task could kick April's morning off to the kind of start he didn't have the strength for today. His will only went so far nowadays, and he needed every bit of it. As predicted, Pigg was waiting for him when he reached the top of the stairs, chubby hands poised on the side of the crib for leverage, as if preparing for a big jump. The child was the happiest he'd ever seen, a bright eyed joy from birth, so much like him it was scary sometimes. He patted his youngest on the head and set up a blanket fort fit for royalty on the floor. It only took a matter of seconds. He'd done this trick every morning for the better part of the tot's life. And as always, he was met with a squeal of approval and the smack of a wet kiss on the side of his face.

April was stirring now, well ahead of schedule. It was going to be that kind of day, where some if not all things were slightly askew.

"What the hell were you up to last night?" The groggy voice came thick and accusing as she sharpened her gaze in the morning light.

He hated that it always started with an accusation, even now.

"Trying to burn me in front of all the people that matter..." She moved sluggishly at first, but like a locomotive out of control built speed and volume as she went on. "That make you feel like a big man? Did it feel good to make me look like a fool?" She bristled past him on the way to the vanity. Even in the company of one she felt the need to dress up. Perhaps she was preparing her battle face. She let out a slicing breath, a pinched blast of air through pursed lips, as if she had a pressure valve. This was always what she did to calm down, when anxiety got the best of her. She did it before an open house or a speech she was about to make. She did it now when she was about to change tack.

"You embarrassed me, Jackson Pollack." She accentuated the name for spite. They both knew he hated that, and that she used it as a reminder of his inadequacies

"All that talk, about some crazy woman... Really! Like you were best friends or something... What was it you said?" She searched for words but he dared not answer, "You said...connected. That was it. You said that you and some crazy old bat that tried to destroy our neighborhood had *connected* in the middle of the Meg-O-Mart."

Her eyes were wide and strange. They threatened to boil over her eyelids and take him to the pits.

"Do you *want* our neighbors to think you're on drugs?"

He definitely didn't have the strength for this conversation, not today. The kids would be waking up. He needed to make breakfast. He needed to be productive.

"Is that what you want?" The words echoed in his ears.

His answer was automatic: "I don't know what came over me," he lied. "I shouldn't have had that last Chardonnay." He put on his most contrite face hoping his false confession would be taken in earnest. Considering she was undoubtedly feeling the consequences of the same indulgence herself, he could pray for lenience just this once.

There was a good chance. Would it be better if he could hold his liquor like a seasoned drinker? She wouldn't want that. And it showed. She drew the brush through her hair, making each strand flawless as her face softened. She still looked like she could be in commercials, even this early in the morning.

"I'm sure the ladies got a kick out of it," she sniffed. She returned her view to the vanity, opening tubs of cream and jars of lotions. She didn't notice that he had left the room.

He heard her laugh, half to herself: "I still don't know what you were thinking."

That was certain.

When he approached the old woman that day he was unsure, his voice small like a child's, tender as a lover's. "*Are you all right, Mrs. MacMillan?*"

She had mouthed the words over and over like the refrain of a song until he'd caught her hands.

They were cold and strong, but frail. But he felt tiny in her grasp, as if he were the delicate one. She was so intense, so alive. She stopped mid-song, as if seeing him for the first time. The recognition was clear.

"You think I'm mad?"

"Mrs. MacMillan," he nodded gently, "you're not mad." He was trying to be kind, and in his heart he didn't believe the old woman was as lost as everyone had made her out to be. He could see strength in her eyes.

"We're all mad here. I'm mad. You're mad." He was transported at once, if it were possible, sucked into the vortex and spit out the other side, blasted straight through space. He was a little boy in a tiny bedroom. On the walls were crayon pictures of fire trucks and magical heroes, flying dragons and posies in a field. He was four years old and listening to a soothing voice read the words for the hundredth time. He knew them by heart. He knew them even now.

"How do you know I'm mad?" He prompted taking the lines from *Alice in Wonderland* as if the past thirty years had been a heartbeat. She made a fine Cheshire cat with those sapphire eyes; they glowed like embers, especially now that they had found him.

"You must be," said the woman, "or you wouldn't have come here."

Lewis Carroll's words reverberated in his ears as the woman's eyes fixed upon his face, twin rabbit holes inviting him to take the leap down and down.

The welt on the woman's face had gone from pink to blazing red in the course of seconds as they spoke. From this close he could smell the source of her pain. There was fertilizer on her hands and face, dusted all over her clothes. Whether or not she could feel it, he couldn't venture a guess.

He brushed the woman's cheek just under the angry weal, as he would Pigg's when the little one bumped an eye or a knee on a sharp table edge. "Mrs. MacMillan, are you all right?"

She answered not as a frail old madwoman but as a knowing trickster. She started a new song, unlike the one before. It rolled off her tongue in a satisfied purr, and followed in confident time. The words dared the world to interrupt. But he wouldn't. Instead he let them fill his head and guide him out of the store and to the task at hand. Now they radiated from his skin onto the canvas as he painted the old woman's eyes.

MRS. RINGHAUS RUNS

*H*er cadence was slow, labored steps that pounded to the ground like fat raindrops. She felt off today, but the entire morning had seemed off-center. She hadn't wanted to run, not really. But there wasn't much choice. There was no escaping the calendar. Each neat box marked what she needed to do with such exquisite clarity that doubt was not possible. That calendar never lied. It assured that every day went according to plan. So today, when the calendar directed her to run, she had complied. It wasn't a sense of duty. The well-marked calendar reminded her that everything had its place and needed to stay where it belonged. But today it mocked her with one simple word: *Easy.*

Nothing was easy. She'd been so looking forward to wearing the new contraption she'd found while flipping through the pages of a magazine, an extravagance she allowed so long as the bills were paid; a bra made of some futuristic polymer, resistant to the heat. It promised all the support she needed, and relief from discomfort. She went without coffee for weeks and skipped her last haircut to make the numbers work. Tripping through the bedroom this morning, she could barely see it. She couldn't make out a hint of color. It just looked metallic, like round silver discs glistening in the dark.

The night was molasses black, speckled with salt stars. When she opened the door, no hint of light came on the horizon. She slogged off the seconds, one slower than the next, in the uncertainty. It was hard enough to change her routine, and now she was doing it blind. The old MacMillan house looked so white it seemed to glow; and eerier still was the silence, worsened by the echoes of her footfalls. In the daylight hours music hung around the Granger house like festive ribbons, leaking out of the windows, curling out of the open door like smoke, but now the only sound was her steps, slow bombs exploding as the neighborhood sat still as a tomb. She had never seen a pothole in Twin Oaks, yet she stepped through the neighborhood hesitantly, as if every few feet a new threat might lurk, something she could not anticipate.

She had pushed the run up a whole hour to ensure she'd be alone. Last time out she'd almost run over poor Wilma Womack. The woman stood there, her hand frozen in a wave, mouth agape half in an utterance of greeting, when Mrs. Ringhaus crashed into her, full on, sweaty body sticking like a bug on a windshield. But the woman hadn't budged. It was as if the collision meant nothing. She stood completely unmoved by what had transpired and carried on as if she were a recorded placed on pause then put back on play. So despite the apprehension that accompanied any departure her routine, Mrs. Ringhaus had rewritten the entire calendar, box by box. She had done so as soon as she'd walked back inside her house. A faint pink smear still remained across every day, like a scar beneath the fresh ink. She hated change, but she hated conflict even more.

It wasn't that she didn't like the woman. She didn't know her well at all. It was a relationship of unspoken hellos and nodding. There was no grudge or offense. But there was a way about that woman that set Mrs. Ringhaus's nerves on end.

Only the Harbages stood between her and the way out now. Their house was the last in the curve before the gate, a bright little cottage with clean white pickets and fresh tufts of daisies sprouting like peach fuzz around the mailbox and front walk. It was a smaller model, not terribly different from hers. Theirs looked like a younger sibling just off to the dance; hers the wise old sister spying from a safe distance. The resemblance was uncanny, if not for the flowers; not that she was comparing. She wasn't like those other women, the ones with their clipboards and contests.

Her walk was trimmed with pink passion begonias. Even now in the moonlight she could see pear-shaped tears clinging to the smooth velvet petals, and if she breathed deeply, she'd pick up the perfume, subtle and distinct, stronger at the doorway than at the gate. They grew more lush and fragrant by the front door. It had taken years to get it that way, three summers if she counted. But she tried not to. It was the one and only project she'd taken on since they had come to the neighborhood.

She saw the Harbages once in a while, walking hand in hand after dinner. They walked up and down the curve, rings twinkling from intertwined fingers. They looked shyly at each other sometimes, like a part of their shared world was still new. She leaned on him a lot, shielding her eyes from the sun, and he touched the small of her back like he cared, and they looked out in front of them like their shared possibilities were as infinite as space. But she was happy to turn the corner and leave that picture behind.

Her steps were not yet effortless, but stronger as she moved further on.

Today it felt like this road might go on forever. From that first baby step, the earth felt transient, her legs wobbly, feet padding at the ground like clumsy paws. She had to adjust, straighten herself and wait for her pulse to quicken, wait for the big push to propel her through the day. It would happen; it always did, at least the past six hundred fifty times she'd gone, every box checked except Sundays. Her least favorite day Sunday cut a white column through every month. But she'd been told before and had learned the hard way: everyone needs a break.

A good run shot her like a rocket into the stratosphere, but the release lacked permanence. That would come if she could just hold on. Nurturing her sense of hope for a turnaround, she told herself it would get better, repeating the mantra as a show of faith. At any rate, the mantra was good company, better than headphones, more reliable than a partner. Beats and breaths, beats and breaths—a rhythm she heard along with the sway of her arms.

'When the day is long and the night/the night is yours alone...'

She could hear it through every exhale. It flooded through her as surely as the oxygen filled her lungs, and it was as involuntary as breathing. It whispered at first, tiny breaths until it swelled inside like a balloon about to burst. But it never went further than the second line. The two repeated as if Michael Stipe and REM had accompanied her on a carousel she could no sooner stop than change her last steps. It's not that she didn't like the song. But a few words can be sinister when set on repeat. It was as if he were singing in her ear. She tried to change the pace, skip a step. But it was no use. The night was hers. Could she even call this morning? It was too early. And there was no doubt she was alone.

Why did it have to be so cold? Was she progressing too slowly? Would the girls forgive her for taking so long? She'd feel better if she could get warm. But this mechanism did more than keep the heat out. It kept the cold in. When she started, all the help forums said she'd feel numb once in a while but today, even after years, she was raw. There was tightness in her chest. It pinched hard around her heart.

'Everybody hurts, sometimes...'

The words flooded in like catastrophe and the world washed away.

She was making out with him to that song on his grandmother's couch. He'd made a tape, a nice slow song to play in the background. They fumbled together, mouths on mouths for the first time, exploring with lips and tongues under the cover of cable TV. As the tune moved over them like water, she knew she loved him even then; even then he was so handsome; gasping for breath in those stolen hours, limbs tangled , hands groping under a patchwork quilt of hearts and tiny birds. They had kept it on them even though it was summer, through the song as it looped and looped again. Three times it had played from start to finish. And when they were through they sipped soda together, and ate popcorn that stuck in his braces.

It felt like forever.

Now, her legs were unsteady, her eyes burned. Her cheeks were damp where the sweat rolled down. It was hard to swallow; her throat felt coarse and dry, as if coated with sand. But she had a plan. She had to stick to the plan.

Her feet were moving beyond her control. Her mind drifted between macadam and the hill ahead, to the light on the horizon trying so hard to break through. The song still ticked in her head like a clock, but things were changing. Stipe was moving on.

'When you're sure you've had enough.'

Mrs. Ringhaus wasn't a quitter.

The morning he'd left there was a note placed underneath her pillow. No apology or consolation. No greeting or conciliatory closing. He didn't sign, as if the shame of seeing both their names together on a page had been too much for him. They had been scribbled in a rush, as if every second counted and he'd already wasted too much time.

This isn't the life I wanted.

It took her several readings for the meaning to congeal. She sat dumbly, hoping the kids wouldn't wake, stifling the groan that came despite efforts to bury it in a pillow. The life he wanted? What did that mean? She sat on the bed they'd just bought, inside the house that still smelled like fresh paint. They'd come so far from that stinky old couch, from proms and braces and long distance letters from school. And the girls were so beautiful. *What didn't he want?*

The next moments were involuntary. There was a noise in the driveway and the baby cried, not a constant cry, but a single wail, like a signal. And she'd dashed outside in her nightgown, embarrassment be damned. She wasn't about to let him cut their life in two with a torn piece of loose leaf. Less than graceful bounding out the door, she stumbled down the first step. He was stooped over something he had dropped when she landed at his feet. He didn't lend a hand as she peeled herself up from the damp earth, brushing dirt from her knees. He just stood there on her new begonias crushed flat under his heels, the car keys in hand.

She regretted her voice to this day, how froglike it had sounded that morning. If only she'd had just another second, she could have cleared her throat. She could've sounded smooth and sincere, like the women in the movies. Instead she croaked, her face puckered in a mass of confusion.

"Where are you going?"

It didn't really matter that he didn't answer. He was going away from her, away from their little girls, and the home she'd worked so hard to make perfect.

She stammered, voice jagged and labored. She was out of breath.

"I can make it how you want it," she insisted, knowing she could if he made a list, if she could see it in front of her.

A pathetic stream of pleas followed that were better received by the smashed flowers, by the oaks in the distance, by the crickets that filled the silence between them. Those were the words she didn't remember as well as what she said last, and his response as he walked away.

"Just give me some more time."

"We don't have any," he said finally.

That was the last that she or the girls had seen of him—three years ago this morning. Her calendar never lied.

Those first years of marriage she had cried where no one could see. She cried into tubs of ice cream, and while she patted out biscuits, and into the washer where no one could hear. She had cried after the baby was born. She cried when he wouldn't touch her, when he wouldn't even look at her.

She was still too soft back then. There wasn't much of that softness left now. She had shed it like a snakeskin.

She was coming up the hill now to the turnaround. Her legs were pumping hard and though it hurt, she pushed. She'd never been good at anything, not like this, not all alone. But she'd worked and she'd planned and now her muscles and body worked together like a machine.

'When you think you've had too much, of this life, well hold on...'

It had been hard not to worry about those poor little flowers at first, those fragile seedlings under all that weight. But with time they were as resilient as she. In time, they'd grown solid on their own, roots planted firmly in the ground, stems strong as they reached for open sky.

She hit the turnaround at full throttle. Only two words boomed in tribal rhythm, and roared in her ears like a battle cry.

'Hold on!'

Dawn broke through the darkness, and Mrs. Ringhaus was heading home.

APRIL'S SHOWER

Sun burned a single beam through the room separating her world from Jack's. He stood at the door watching as if there were anything else to be said and she, if but for a second, felt a twinge of sympathy for the man. But it was no matter now. He'd gone, taking all that foolishness down the hall with him. He was sorry, as always, but it stunk where he stood of ineffectiveness and regret. It was stale.

April tried to inhale slowly, calming her nerves, picking through several crystal decanters she kept on the vanity. She put her hands high on her forehead as she did when the headaches kicked in and pulled at her scalp so all the skin went taut. Even in this awful light the benefits of her salt peel were nothing short of miraculous. She was radiant. It took the sting from the unpleasantness, a trade she would have to accept for now. From a slender bottle she poured a touch of lavender on the tips of her fingers and let them settle just under her nose as she murmured softly the words she'd been told to recite when the stress became too much. Nothing was more tragic than stress lines.

"*A cane scottato l'acqua fredda pure calda. A malie estremi non mancano modi.*" The words bubbled on her tongue like fine caviar and slid themselves over her lips as she let them linger there before repeating. They didn't mean much to her now but they would when they took hold. Who said you have to suffer to be beautiful?

She held tightly to her robe as the gooseflesh on her arms and legs bloomed like flowers in the spring. The louvered doors slid open with a hiss and in seconds she was in territory that was hers and hers alone. Though it was summer it was cold; not cold, but frigid. She'd read in *Interiors Superior* that keeping the temperature low would keep her leathers supple, her chiffons light, and her satins shining. But she didn't need a magazine to tell her that. She preferred a chill.

By any other's estimation this would be considered a room, and a sprawling one at that. *Closet* was so crude. It implied hiding, smallness, cramped quarters where dirty socks were shoved. But this was a palace meant for a queen. It wasn't some cubby for hide-and-seek, as the children had learned. It wasn't a dumping ground sullied with balled up t-shirts or knick-knacks, but rows and columns in perfect balance, a sanctuary from the chaos outside. When she was in here even gentle Pigg knew to cry elsewhere.

The far wall was a two-tiered tribute to organization, a monument in gold divvied into lots, not simply by hue, but by pattern, fabrics and season. Today she went right for the yellows, bright but not too bright. She passed the metallics by. They'd look gauche with her tan. She breezed by a party dress in warm tangerine and a saffron short set to a pale suit that reminded her of whipped butter. It was barely a touch lighter than her own hair and brought out the flecks of sunlight that danced in her eyes. She knew it was the case without looking but it felt damn good to have the mirror remind her. She looked good in the gilded frame, even in her slinky bathrobe. She was slim, tight and razor sharp. The luncheon wasn't for hours, but she would need every second to prepare. A lot went into being April Pollack.

She had an hour at least until the kids would stir. The one good thing about the long summer nights was the longer summer mornings. And Jack would tend to them. He was good at that. Everything had a way of balancing that way. There was ample time to line up her garments on the bed in the order she would put them on, enough time to peel and scrub away the old face, to drink a slurry of fresh fruits and herbs. Annabelle said they had miracle qualities. April knew it had more to do with antioxidants. It was like Mr. Hayes had said years ago in geometry: *there is no magic solution.* Long term problems needed long term work, and she was prepared to put it in. Just like a good theorem, her morning routine was a fixed list of precise steps.

"Good morning!" A toothless relic with raisin eyes hopped up on the four poster bed. Amid the plump, overstuffed pillows he looked like a plucked chicken, fragile and thin. He purred once and then shivered, as was his way. Hairless cats didn't shed, which meant they didn't leave hair on delicate frocks. He nosed her bra as if on command, pushing it toward her when she'd finished steaming a pair of lace panties and white thigh-high stockings. "You are such a good helper."

Jack had never heard her talk this way, and the low coo of her voice was not familiar even to her own children, but only to Sol the cat. She trusted him with all of her secrets, enough to stand sentry while she did what needed to be done. She knew he'd never tell.

The master bath was the reason she had chosen this home. The Gabled Homestead was a model of amenities, but it wasn't the picture window in the front sitting room or the cathedral ceilings in the dining room that drew April's attention. It wasn't even the widow's walk in Pigg's nursery as Jack had thought. They were all nice, of course, in the way that a pretty flower in a man's lapel is lovely if it's in the lapel of an Armani. The Homestead had everything a young couple could want. But it was the master bath that set it apart from all the others in Twin Oaks, especially in April's eyes.

The oversized tub was set three steps up, in fine Italian marble, with water jets that blew furious bubbles on aching backs and gentle streaming fingers over aching bones. But what seemed to call to her today was through the archway dividing the room.

The steam shower was meant for two. If she had to guess, three people could fit inside the clear glass hollow with room to spare. But she enjoyed being alone. She ran a hand over the cool whites and creams that fringed the smooth, round door. What kind of artist can't appreciate inlaid tile imported from Ireland? Jack thought the whole project was overkill, but April knew there was no such thing. The inside walls were dark as the ripest plums and offset the cool surroundings. Once inside, it was like she was somewhere else altogether. It was that way by design.

The hot jets warmed the back of her neck as the others sputtered steam and gentle rushes of water over her body. She thumbed a gray container from the ledge, smearing its rough contents over her legs, as Abigail had instructed. She said the Himalayan salts and Hawaiian muds would slough away age and bring back the bounce to her supple legs. It stung, but the pain would be tempered by the results. The lawns chairwoman had promised. The gloppy mix of pinkish browns and old dried-up berry smelled to high heaven and burned like hell, but in the end it was worth the sacrifice. Jack could never understand that.

"You want to name our baby Pigg?" He'd looked at her with that half-cocked grin, one eyebrow raised. She wanted to punch him when he did that. He thought it was charming, harkening back to their younger days. It wasn't charming then either.

"It's sexless, remember?" She said it flatly, hating to explain it, the first time as much as the twenty-sixth time. As if she needed to justify her own thoughts... But she relented, and went over it yet again in slow words so he'd understand. It was like a song by the time the ink on the birth certificate had dried, and by then it seemed as though she'd sung it a hundred times.

"We're not doing that to Pigg!" she'd said as the gifts came rolling in, dolls and kitchens, footballs and blocks, all with nudges as to which one the child should pick. "Why is it so important that the baby be a girl or a boy?" She insisted against either.

A study in Sweden said the roles could be stifling, that gender was a fluid thing if you let it be. She had read that as many times as she'd been asked. And it had struck a chord. Her favorite teacher, Mr. Hayes, used to say that two halves made a whole no matter how you stacked them. She'd always loved him for that.

"Why should one word have so much power?" He had no answer. He stared blankly and relented as he did for reasons that had nothing to do with Sweden or studies.

She squeezed oil out of a slim silver tube. It was fragrant like cardamom pods and vanilla. And as instructed she began rubbing it into her calves, above her knee, and beyond her thigh. Annabelle was at least a decade older than April and had legs like a thoroughbred. She had sworn by this ritual when she'd given her the tiny tube. It was warm to the touch, much like the mud, warmer still than the steamy water, growing hottest as it hit her skin, a sensation that wasn't particularly unpleasant.

When she and Jack were younger he would paint well into the night and she'd stay at his side watching as he mixed oils, making his dreams come to life right in front of her eyes. They would order takeout and eat by candlelight, the tiny apartment aglow with the only light source they could afford. They'd sit cross-legged on the floor, spooning bites of rice into each other's mouths like god and goddess. They were playful and fearless. She dared him to eat a ghost pepper one night and he did it just because she'd said so. Now she couldn't get him to shut up about an old lady in the Meg-O-Mart.

He was so hot then. He still was. He certainly had that going for him, didn't he?

She took a purple bottle from the shelf and squeezed the gel inside into the palm of her hand. Tiny bubbles caught the light and glittered there. They wiggled as if suspended in water like tiny jellyfish. Abigail said it would tighten her belly and make her skin gleam like treasure.

It was alchemy that changed her skin to gold; it all boiled down to simple chemical reactions. She knew that. Mr. Hayes taught her well enough in high school chemistry, that everything boiled down to simple chemical reactions: beauty, love, sex, even power were all part of that delicious balance that hangs in the hands of simple chemistry. A baby is a girl until a few hormones in the womb call him otherwise. A few clicks of serotonin in the system and a young kid will fall in love. It had less to do with long dark eyelashes and more to do with pheromones. She knew that. And chemicals never lied.

The purple goo was pliant and cool. It smelled of lavender and bergamot. She rubbed it into her abdomen and felt the bubbles pop against her skin. There was a similar burn. But again it wasn't entirely unpleasant.

When they were young she and Jack would roll around on the floor like animals. He'd leave her panting and he'd collapse in a heap at her side. They'd talk until sunrise about their dreams, about philosophy and art. He said he was going to give her the world and she damn near melted.

But junkies say shit like that all the time.

She'd had to tie him down those first three nights when it had gone too far. She wiped his head with a washcloth and caught his sick in a basin at his side. And she never once left him, not to sleep or to eat. She peed with the door open and talked to him all the while, just as a mother would to a toddler who couldn't bear to stand at a closed door. She never broke his gaze once, not even in those strange times. She gritted her teeth and talked through the sweats and the shaking and all the high and mighty curses. He'd never promised those hours of grief. But she got them.

When they were adventurous, he would blindfold her and feed her fresh berries. Once he used the candles, all up and down her belly. It wasn't so bad. In fact, it was quite the opposite once she let herself go completely. The heat stung and cooled as he said it would. She gave him that trust. It sizzled down the length of her, going dead cold just beneath her navel.

His eyes were so intense. They devoured her when they were together. But now when she saw him she saw the sad sweating wraith that wouldn't let her pee, that awful stinking mess. She saw what he could be, ruined.

The bubbling concoction tingled on her skin. She was all slick and foamy. She'd like to tie him up again, now, some night when the kids were tucked away, now that he was healthy. She'd tie him up so he couldn't disappear out back when he thought she wouldn't notice. She'd tie up those strong arms of his behind his back so he couldn't do a thing. He'd have to sit there and take it. She'd pull one of her scarves tight against his wrists and straddle him face to face. She'd stare into those eyes until they came back to her.

But she knew that that road would get her nowhere.

Her hands glided and she gave into the inevitable. She stroked and caressed his face, the face that was nothing if not handsome still. She dug her fingers hard into his neck and kissed the stubble on his chin. She kissed his cheeks and his forehead all over his face, building in passion until she kissed him full and deep, searching as she did for those god and goddess days on the floor. She nipped at his earlobes and nibbled until she caught on something amiss behind his ear. Like a fuzzy ball on a sweater, it jutted out and she pulled it between her teeth, but it wouldn't give. She squared herself on top of him and pulled with all her might, yanking and pulling until finally the skin gave like a mask. She peeled it up and off of the tied man for what seemed an eternity, until all that remained was the new man sitting beneath her. Mr. Hayes, with his concentrating look, the soft-spoken chemistry teacher with the side-swept hair, wriggled beneath her, his crystal gray eyes penetrating her as they had almost twenty years ago.

And they still did the trick, a secret only she and the wrinkled beast ever shared.

"Solomon," she whispered. She was close to finished here, all the jars and tubes nearly exhausted. Yet she wasn't through.

She grabbed the detachable shower head and sat where the steam, thick as cotton, billowed and swirled like a beckoning hand in the air. She had fantasized about making love to Solomon in every room of the school. Chemistry was a long, drawn-out period, meant for experiments. As Mr. Hayes spoke in his honey voice about electrical explosions, April's hands would disappear under the dark confines of the high lab table for some research of her own. She imagined their tongues and lips twisting together over colloid lecture, imagining any minute she could get him alone. Mr. Hayes would look over as she let out a gasp that she blamed on pure scientific enthusiasm. But she could tell by the pink in his cheeks that he'd known exactly what she'd done. She was a dirty girl that way.

Results on average varied between three to five minutes. She kept it to herself. She held it in, so close.

But something was off today.

The showerhead sputtered. Her mind wandered. She wanted dessert all of a sudden. It was that vanilla smell, like cake. At her baby shower Agnes had wheeled out an extravagant sponge-filled with lemon curd and key lime custard. No one understood what April was doing, with her subtle greens and neutral yellows, not even the women of her association. Abigail yawned and Annabelle toyed with a busboy named Franco. Agnes networked. Even Mrs. MacMillan, who already had a faraway and perhaps disoriented look, seemed baffled by the whole silly affair.

Standing across the room and smiling as she fielded question after question about pinks and blues, Mrs. Granger inclined her head slightly. She was a tall, stately woman with the posture of a pontiff and the carriage of a king. The president of the association was a woman who knew what she wanted and how to get it. She was so confident and set in everything she did, her eyes like molten steel. She took long slinking steps that floated on water. She touched her fingers to April's; it had felt like lightning in an ice storm. She'd looked long and hard at the younger woman and leaned in close when she spoke. She'd whispered her message when no one was around. The others prattled on about bows or baseballs, but Mrs. Granger had interest in neither. April couldn't remember the entire conversation now, or if the business at hand was a house sale or yard issue that started it off. But she could feel the words that came against her ears, faint breaths just less than audible, pressing one after another until at last she'd let them in. She had needed something that day: something important. And that's exactly what it was, warm against her skin they mingled, the need and want melding together in a beautiful rhythmic song. They swam inside her and filled her like a balloon ready to burst. And then Mrs. Granger spoke one phrase so true and clear that it rang through her like a church bell, resounding in her ears and shaking her bones: "I need you to be my vice."

And with that, April was complete.

TITAN

*"D*ear, when you go out today you need to get the car washed, all right?"

Agnes still spoke to him as if he was nine years old, the singsong sound of a reminder to wash behind his ears or finish his broccoli. She was fiddling with a large diamond stud. It stuck out from her ear like a tumor.

"What?"

Last night he was up late, and his pupils were finding it hard to adjust to the morning sun, so very different than the soft gentle glow of his computer downstairs. He hadn't even breached the threshold of the new day and already she'd rattled off the beginnings of three separate and completely unrelated conversations. He hadn't caught one. But now she stood with the sun at her back, head tilted his way, waiting for the response she demanded.

"I was planning on staying around here today. I have a lot that needs to be done."

She breezed by as if he'd not spoken, grabbing her atomizer from the powder blue clutch at her side, spraying twice decisively on each side of her delicate neck. She gave her cheeks two quick pinches, looking long in the entranceway mirror, and when she was satisfied pulled a long thin sheath of paper rolled tight like prison messages from the small hidden pocket inside her skirt. But this was no secret. Her "must do list" was an unending list of chores fit for a titan and growing exponentially with every passing day. She patted it into his hand and conspiratorially lowered her once melodic voice to the barest whisper filled with one note gravity.

"Adam, there is poo on your car."

Her eyes were wide and clear and as chilly as her crisp, clean suit.

"Oh, I know." He exhaled as if blowing a party balloon across the hall. "It must've happened yesterday. I think there is a pair of crows hanging out around those trees."

He knew this was wrong.

"Since yesterday? Adam, really. *That's* been sitting in our driveway where people can see it for over a day." She wasn't shrill, not yet. But he knew she'd get there if he let her. "What will people think? You need to get to the car wash today—as soon as you can."

"I'll go today, Mom; enjoy your luncheon."

"Breakfast, dear." Her shoulders slackened and the edge went out of her voice. "It's a breakfast. A meeting, really. I'm just finalizing some plans with the Rutherfords. They're over in Solemn Pines across the highway."

He rubbed his head with a small shrug of his shoulders.

"A whole new development, Adam; all those new homes... Everyone's talking about them. It could mean dozens of new clients. The *right* kind!" Her eyes twinkled hungrily as she ticked off the possibilities, finger to finger. "The Lark Meadow, the Arbor Isle. They have a new one that's twice the size of the Grandview. Can you imagine?" She straightened her jacket, running both hands down the seam at her belly. "I can't say I'm looking forward to seeing all those goodies laid out. So tempting... But I've got to save my credits for the luncheon, dear. If I eat melon and water all day, I have forty-three *sometimes credits* left for the afternoon. And that will be worth it."

"I don't understand why you do this to yourself anyway, Mom. You look great."

She smoothed the skin under his eyes as if he were still thirteen, always making sure he was perfect though they both knew it was a stretch. He was bleary-eyed, fighting a headache and the bleached perfection of the marble hall was on the verge of making him ill. He kept his head down. Sun poured in through the kitchen window as if it were a giant magnifying glass. He felt like a bug.

He wasn't the type to give false praise, and his mother wasn't the type to take it. She did indeed look good, as did everything else Agnes Moore touched. The house was meticulous, her suit a product of the utmost coordination and design. Her hair fell in pristine symmetrical waves; her chin framed her precisely-made face. Her teeth were straight and white when she smiled. She brightened but darkened almost in the same instant.

"You know, dear, I do appreciate you coming back here to help; I mean, all you're doing with, well, you know..."

They both knew she couldn't say it. Neither of them had yet.

"I need to stop at Calliope's today to pick up the cake for the luncheon. They do those cakes like on TV. It's going to be something really special. And I'm in charge of that, so that's where I need to be."

There was pleading beneath the prattling only he could pick up, like an undertone on an old fashioned record.

"Listen, I got it, Mom; pills at 10:30. Then the nurse comes. I'll ask Mr. Chalmers if he gave any thought to that box thing. I got the lawn. I got the mail. I got the flowerbeds. I got it."

For a second he could see relief flood in underneath all that precision, and the color return to her cheeks for the first time in weeks.

"Flyers to Mrs. Granger?"

"I got it, Mom. I'll hit her on the way to Mr. Strings."
She shrugged.

Mr. Chalmers lived in the White Briar Chalet, a quaint Tudor throwback at the other end of the loop. He had become a thorn in his mother's proverbial paw.

"That house could be a show piece, if he'd let it shine."

"Mom, I got it. Go enjoy your luncheon. Knock 'em dead, okay?"

She knew what she was capable of, but it was good to hear him say it. He was still her little boy, hair sticking out every which way, tiny tufts of cocoa fuzz. She missed him sometimes. And he missed her too. She was sure of it.

They both tried not to think about the man two floors up. The wound was still fresh, and if they put the words out between them, it would it be a tangible thing; the nightmare of what was happening would become all the more real.

"And the poop dear?"

He looked at the list and saw his day spread out like fog before his eyes. Despite twenty-four years to the contrary, he shrugged boyishly.

"Even if I have to wash it myself..."

"I don't know what I'd do without you, Adam."

"I know." He smiled, partly because he could hear the last hiss of steam that meant his cup was almost full and there was nothing better than the first sip of coffee on a day like today. But he smiled mostly because she was right. His mother had a way with words. She worked her magic and most folks were warm clay in her hands. He had no doubt in his mind that she would go into that meeting and come back with contracts to do the entire Pines neighborhood. She disappeared out the great entryway in a blue streak.

"Go get 'em," he called.

"Forty-three credits, dear. I can't wait!" she returned over her shoulder.

He didn't want to think about 10:30, or the hours

before. Those he buried in the place in his brain where he kept things like lost keys and sneakers never to be found again. When Hettie came in her white van he was free to step out and put *upstairs* behind him. By then the cords of his neck pulled hard at the back of his head. The sun was welcome on his bare arms like a salve on tender muscles, hot and cold and all relief from a pain he couldn't describe. He didn't know why he ached. The heaviness wasn't physical. But he felt like he carried the world on his shoulders. Though his eyes burned like a cat had pissed in them, he stared into the sky, as cloudless and blue as in a children's storybook. He enjoyed this time of day, especially when it was as clear as it was right now. He'd learned how quickly the clouds could roll in and change the horizon.

Mr. Chalmers house stuck out from the others, even from this distance. Topsy-turvy towers of crumpled brown flanked the path to his front door. If the large picture windows were the eyes of the home, they were more than certainly the color of chocolate milk, obscured completely by craggy boxes and picture frames covered in craft paper. It drove the ladies in the society to the brink of madness, the way this man disregarded bulk trash day and the basic tenets of good recycling. Adam loved every bit of it.

"Strings!"

He walked in without knocking, nearly tripping over a half-painted rocking horse. The older man was crouched on the ground, a paintbrush held between his teeth like a tango rose."

"We missed you this morning, kid."

On Adam's second day back he'd taken a stroll through Twin Oaks. That was when he'd heard the Spanish guitar coming from Mr. Chalmers' house, and it was also the first day he came to visit. He hadn't stopped visiting since.

"Makin' this for little Lucy." The old man didn't look away from the horse. He squinted his eyes so tight that it was hard to tell where his forehead ended and his brow began. He turned himself parallel to the wooden face, adding just the right highlight to its candy pink lips. They glistened as if to be kissed. "You know, Dawn's girl."

Adam's face warmed. He felt like he should be helping.

"Sorry, Strings, I had some things to do."

The older man crept up first to his knees and then to his feet. His words were deliberate. "How is your dad doing, kiddo?"

Those hours that he didn't want to think about fought against the surface of his mind, the smell of antiseptic, the thick metal stitches separating pieces of skull, those thin chicken legs poking out of the yellow quilt like some obscene cartoon.

"He's, uh. He's... Shit Benny. He's not fine. I'm not going to say that anymore. I'd say he's in good spirits, or he's fighting the good fight. But it's not a good fight. A month ago he was fine. And now he's dying. And he knows it."

These mornings with Ben Chalmers had always been good for him, even when he was a little boy and the neighborhood was his, and the old Macmillan house, long before developments and committees and words like eyesore or blight, had resembled Grey Gardens.

Ben patted the young man on the arm as he would his own son. There weren't words for times like these. Instead, he wove through three stacks of boxes toward the couch, pulled up his black Stratocaster and began to play.

It was a slow, tuneful song that poured through the house. It shook the panes of glass shielded behind craft paper, old paintings no doubt hiding their expressions, unable to conceal how the music moved them.

Adam walked to the other side where his stool was already waiting, took a deep breath and sat down. He lay his chin to his chest letting all those hours flow out through his fingers in a steady heartbeat that brought them both back to life.

As they'd done years ago, and as for the past month,

they jammed until the heaviness turned to light.

"You're sweet on her, you know."

"What?"

"Don't play dumb, boy; it doesn't suit you. That girl Dawn and you. There's something there, and don't you say there ain't. Ain't no worse thing you can do than deny the spark."

He raised his eyebrows at the man who ignored it like a gnat or telemarketer.

"The spark, right there in the eyes, like electricity. It's there every time you two are in a room together, right there for the whole world to see. Zap, just like that!"

"Benny, are you high?"

The old man laughed. "Not since 1963, friend. Bea would have my head. I ain't high." He walked over to Adam, laughing as he went. "But I'm right."

There was a reason that Adam regretted being late today that went further than punctuality or duty. He'd secretly timed his journeys to run into her (accidentally) from the very first time it had happened a month ago.

"Uh, maybe," he shrugged. "But another time, Strings. I've got about a thousand things to do on the big list today. Time is running against me."

"Ah, the list..." Mr. Chalmers stretched. "I suppose they want me to do something with the boxes, again."

Adam hated doing these jobs for his mother, especially when it meant messing with someone he respected.

"Actually," he read from the paper, "the Grounds and FaÃ§ades committee is planning a neighborhood yard sale that you may be interested taking part in..." His voice trailed as he eyed the old man over the paper. "Actually, Agnes would like to know if you have any collectibles that you may be willing to sell to her for repurposing, for her decorating. I'm sure she'll pay you a fair price."

Chalmers laughed heartily. "Boy, I've got to hand it to you, you're some messenger. Tell your mom I'll get a few boxes ready for her. I'm sure Bea will be happy to be rid of some of these old records, maybe some of the *Rock Gods*. I've got about seventy back issues, give or take, that I can pass her way."

"Really?"

The old man had battled with Agnes for years over his clutter and now was working with her, no questions asked.

"Really," he winked. "I've got three big shipments coming in this week. I've got to make some space."

When Adam left he'd promised Strings that they could revisit the 'Dawn discussion' if Strings would promise to keep his home shopping purchases down to a minimum, at least for the next few weeks.

After that, he ticked through the to do's in double-time, whistling while he finished the lawn, taking extra care with a set of bulbs he split and wrapped for planting. He even took care of the poop situation. Looping out past the highway for a hot wax, he stopped for a milkshake on his way back. But he regretted that decision as soon as he turned into the gates, because he'd left her for last.

Almost everyone enjoyed a visit to Mrs. Granger's stately home, especially in the afternoon. But Adam dreaded the woman, and her house even more. Something about it gave him the creeps. That music in the afternoon and the weird cinnamon smell never made him think of theme parks or Christmas villages as the women in the society had always joked. For him, it was more *Hansel and Gretel*, or a Venus flytrap waiting for a tasty beetle to scuttle by.

It was well past three o'clock, but the house was silent. He'd forgotten that she was at the luncheon with his mother. More than likely she was eating designer cakes and ripping apart the good folks of the neighborhood who were unable to attend. He could slip up the path and leave the flyers wedged between the storm door and front doors. As childish as it seemed, he envisioned himself getting caught there, like a bee stuck between windowpanes, wedged in glass for the entire neighborhood to see. He practically ran down the walk until he was safe on the street again. It was funny how a grown man could be reduced to infancy by the thought of an old woman and her off-kilter house and perfect gardens.

This was so far from where he was this spring, before the Earth shifted to heaven and his life had turned inward. A month ago he had an army of lackeys who would have been doing all this for him if he'd asked, and most of the time even if he didn't. He had a house that made Mrs. Granger's look like a shed. He had properties and cars. Models and starlets were getting him into VIP rooms where rappers knew his name. He had everything anyone could ever want, just as he realized he didn't. The call came from Agnes after he'd hit his millionth download: *Dad fell,* she'd said.

It never ceased to amaze him how quickly it all had happened. He was in his cube one day at Rokware, the software giant, working on his own game. It took him days into nights to lay out the labyrinths alone, getting the mazes and point of view just right. He was killing himself to get it to the beta testers. It had been little more than a whim when he did it, for kicks, putting the app together so he and the other programmers could have a laugh. It had only taken a lunch hour to do it. Who knew a stupid tool that let people draw moustaches on other people's pictures was going to be his legacy? The damn thing had taken over before he knew it. The acclaim and dignity that followed could never have been foreseen. It made *Titan's Reign* disappear. This one stupid thing had become his damned fortune. He'd become *moustache man.* How the mighty could fall in seconds.

It was a joke.

The truth had only occurred to him when Agnes called a month ago, just after he'd been told *StashYou!* had hit the top. *Dad fell,* she'd said, giving no hint of what that actually meant. She never said the word 'malignant', only that he needed to come home, and she never said the word 'terminal', not even when his flight had landed later that evening. The doctors had laid out the prognosis, and then they'd called him a model son for the way he'd dropped an *empire* to move back home. They had called him 'admirable', and 'nothing short of heroic', and spoke his name with an air of nobility, as if any of that mattered. What they didn't know was that he'd planned to let it go all along. It was all too much to bear.

He enjoyed it here working through the night far under the world where no one could touch him; he never once missed his high rise view. He relished the quiet that came long after the world slept. He wore that silence like a warm cloak around his shoulders, basking in the soft iridescence, only the clicks of the keyboard in his ears. They lulled his mind to calm when the world came crashing in and when the questions came prying. It was Adam alone with his maze, forging forward in the shadows, one step after the next with no thought of time or what happens when it runs out. It didn't matter whether he was powerful or successful or rich. In the end it was always one man in the dark. He thought of that most nights and let his mind drift to the simple things, one click to the next, until dawn draped over the sky. With every second he'd wait for that light.

DAWN BREAKS

*H*er steps were quick now, fluid. She was warmed up and beyond the hardest hill, easing home without the weight of the past. It coursed through her veins like venom, this feeling she'd lost for years. It singed her skin where the air and sweat met, sizzling like electricity. What would her girls think if they saw her this way, soaked, skin steaming against this early air? She was soaring through it, gliding in an invisible plane, the lasso of truth draped around her waist. She was an Amazon. Did it count as daydreaming if the sun wasn't up yet? Things like that didn't fit in her schedule, but for the first time in ages she couldn't give a damn about what the calendar said. Her mind drifted and she felt light on her feet, like she could go forever. Michael wasn't haunting her now and neither was time.

A few years could mean so much.

She was tougher and harder and well-defined now, thanks to discipline and routine. Yet there were still a few curves. Some of the softness from years ago remained, a soft cushion left over for safekeeping. She hadn't thought about it before, but she might just look all right in one of those expensive nightgowns in the catalogs that came every other week. She denied herself so much, didn't she?

Yes, she'd worked hard to get where she was.

She pulled at the clasp at the back of her new running bra. It was cold to the touch but the rest of the fabric felt as if it were burning where the seam met her hot skin. It cut into her flesh like a chastity belt. Yes, she definitely had some curves to spare.

This was so new, like nothing she'd allowed herself before. The ad had said that it would be cool and supportive, but she hadn't considered that it might be lovely too. But it was so uncomfortable. And she was so awkward. How did the women in the magazines do it?

When all the bills were paid and the kids had their shoes and class pictures and lunchtime snacks, sometimes she would indulge herself with a magazine. Not those tabloids—she wouldn't take gossip for free—but a *Runner's Monthly* or a nutrition guide she'd snatch off the shelf as soon as she saw them. Once she bought a tribute to the late Johnny Cash, just because his sad eyes spoke volumes to her, more so than any mournful song. But a few weeks ago she bought a ladies' magazine, the kind that talks about the big secret to turning guys on, and the big secret to "Keeping That Spark". Why did everything have to be such a secret? And according to the magazine it wasn't that big a mystery anyhow. They both had the same answer, and it was a pretty obvious guess. She'd laughed in spite of herself. It was all dumb really, and almost nine dollars to boot. For that she could have gotten Lucy that new monster doll, the one with the glow-in-the-dark skin. But leafing through the perfume ads and the article about kissing styles, she felt the blood rush to her face. A blush came to her cheek. She'd never admit it this anyone, not even her girls when they were old enough to understand, but a little part of her knew it was worth it—the Moving Beauty TruFit Luxury Sports bra.

Just call me Dawn, she'd said. She could just smack herself. If she could turn back the clock, she would. *Dawn,* like she was some teenage girl. Who does that?

His eyes were so dark that they were hard to read, and when he looked at her she could only see how nervous she was reflected in them. He was there every day for the pickup, the young man helping out at the Chalmers place. Adam. He couldn't be more than twenty-four or twenty-five. She had a dress from high school in the back of her closet that was just about that age, give or take a year. It was so silly to entertain such a thought...

She took a deep breath and shrugged her shoulders. Sometimes that helped when the edges of her old bra pinched her skin. She'd shrug a few times and shake her hands out like a boxer before a fight and everything would fall back into place. But the 'Fit' hugged her tightly, as if it were part of her skin. She was moving quickly now, and Twin Oaks was approaching.

There was a protocol for everything. She had lists for household chores and a checklist for her pantry and cupboards. By the day of the week she could tell you what colors went into the wash and whether they were eating pasta or chicken for dinner. But she'd dropped all that when she'd uttered those two words without a thought: *Just Dawn,* as if she were some kind of lounge act or exotic dancer with nothing but a first name. Now he was there every day with his music and that faraway look, with those eyes that seemed sad even when he smiled, those eyes that ripped through the moment to look for something beyond what was right in front of him.

He'd looked like a young boy to her that first day in the Chalmers' sitting room. He played with Becca and Lucy on an old beat-up keyboard, and they loved his lively song. He was so kind to the girls, and pleasant to her, too. And of course he was a good looking, but she hadn't been looking then, at least not on a conscious level. Somewhere inside she was sure she'd taken note of those wide-set shoulders and long lean arms, the way he seemed to glide from one instant to the next so effortlessly, and how he shifted back to self-awareness the second his fingers stopped moving. He was soft-spoken, gentle. She had never been good at small talk, and probably came across as off-putting when he made attempts at conversation. She bristled by him on her way to the next room in search of water.

That first day had turned into every morning, many of which were non-events. She'd breeze by the two of them playing music, Mr. Chalmers wrapped in a world of six-strings, Adam wailing away on a drum solo. Sometimes they'd play the saddest songs she'd ever heard, songs that felt like they held her down with all the weight of the world.

Or she might see him in the neighborhood, loading things into the car for his mother. Dawn didn't like to judge, but she seemed to be one of those women that had all the trappings of a crayon woman, bright smile that scowled behind overly white teeth, perfect style and empty eyes.

Yet this was never about crayons, but sparks. Years ago, Michael had said so when he'd offered his confession, and she'd wanted nothing more than to bury him deep in the earth. She'd been with him for the better part of her life, and suddenly he'd had the gall to talk about sparks? It had made no sense to her, not then.

Yesterday she'd come in all huff and sweat, as always, and there he was, tall and lean with those bad news eyes turned down; gentle, sad eyes that had met hers for an intentional moment. And she hadn't expected her stomach to lurch when he stood up, but it had, with a vengeance, as if the floor had fallen out beneath her. When those eyes met hers and he held out his hand, it was like all gravity disappeared. Her breaths came as quickly as the pace of her last steps, and she hoped that no one noticed that she'd flushed for the first time in years. How embarrassed she felt, blushing so when his voice, rich beyond his age, spoke.

"We haven't been formally introduced. I'm Adam."

"I'm..." Her voice caught in her throat, "...sweating all over."

His smile was bright and natural, like he'd heard something amusing. He wiped his hand on his shorts and shrugged as if to say he didn't mind.

"You're like Atalanta." He smiled, and there it was again, bright and warm as the best summer day.

"Sorry?"

"From mythology... She was abandoned on a mountain and raised by a bear, which led to her being a pretty fierce hunter. She was the fastest woman in mythology. No man could catch her, not even the fastest, strongest warriors. But they all admired her, of course. They'd lay down their lives for her, literally, racing to the death for a chance at her love. Finally, this guy Hippomenes came along, who decided to challenged her." Adam took a big step backward and his voice drifted with him down the narrow hallway to the other room.

"What happened?"

She fanned her hands feverishly hoping these few seconds would give her some time to air out before he emerged in the doorway.

"He cheated to win. He begged Aphrodite to help and she gave him three golden apples." He handed her a chilled bottle of high-end water. "They were supposed to be irresistible. So he threw them on the course to distract her."

"Did it work?"

He held his hands up in a surrendering shrug, and tilted his head with a devilish grin.

"Not very fair..."

"She ended up really liking him. They became passionate lovers." Then he added with a thought, "Physically and spiritually."

"A happy ending, hmmm... I don't know much about

mythology, but isn't there usually a twist?" She drank greedily.

"They were both turned into lions by a goddess that got mad at them for making love in one of her temples."

As the quiet settled between them, she realized. "Aphrodite."

His smile widened as she made the connection. "And there's the curveball." As if catching himself, he cocked his head, no longer devilish, but apologetic. "I'm really into my myths. Sorry if I bored you, Mrs. Ringhaus."

"Oh, I'm not bored at all; quite the opposite." She wasn't sure if she'd remembered to breathe during his story. She dried her hand as best she could and hoped she'd stopped dripping.

A strange croaking sound came from her mouth, and before she knew it those words had come out like belches: "Dawn," her voice cracked like a teenaged girl. "Just call me Dawn." He shook her hand and his warmth seemed to radiate up through her arm all the way to her eyelids. Inside, she was spinning like a ballerina in a pirouette, yet her body remained grounded to the spot where she stood. Her heartbeat pounded inside her ears.

Of course she was old enough to know better. And she had the girls to think about, too. But the way he looked at her had stirred something she'd all but forgotten, or perhaps never known. He'd leaned in very close to hear what she'd said, and she could smell the soap on his skin, the faint scent of shampoo. But it was his heat that she could feel on her face and neck.

"I forgot to cool down," she shouted as if she'd left something on the stove, her house in imminent danger of burning to the ground. She backed out the door quickly, so quickly in fact that he could not answer, and ran full speed toward the street, almost trouncing poor Wilma Womack who was once more and forever walking her all-too-intelligent, and fiercely handsome, dog.

The embarrassment alone was enough to kill her, so

taking matters into her own hands she interrupted her routine with an unprecedented day off in the middle of the week. She'd even pushed up her run today to this ungodly hour to avoid any threat of worsening whatever damage she'd done. Her protocol, her schedule, the way she operated each and every day had all changed in one instant.

But it was beautiful now, wasn't it? Barreling through the gates of Twin Oaks, with the mauve and purple flowering plants above, it looked as if the sun would join her for this last leg. Her toes barely touched the ground, rotating like wheels as she flew forward to her goal, and she could only wonder if every morning that she'd run had been as it was right now. Or had she just ignored the splendor, the cadence? Crickets, birds and breeze met at once in a symphony that drove her faster and harder with each heartbeat. Ringlets of sun dangled in the air like bangles. Hints of gold peeked through a clear new sky. A single, devilish cloud hung overhead, full and plump and cinched at the middle like an hourglass. It winked coyly at her like a pinup watching from above. She could feel herself bouncing back by the second. She'd missed so much. And it was a perfect return.

Then something snapped. It was almost automatic, the way her fingers found the clasp. As it had clung to her in defeat, it now popped like a party favor, releasing her in victory. So she *was* Atalanta after all. She let it dangle, enjoying the rhythmic wave of the shiny fabric against her skin, a flag of conquest, a badge. The cool air touched her bare skin, which all but screamed in relief. She flipped the metallic strap under one finger and flung it onto the sidewalk.

Her steps were no longer feverish but meditative through the loop she'd taken every day for longer than she'd like to remember. Things were different this morning. The grass didn't just smell fresh, it smelled alive. Bulbous drops of dew hung on the limbs and leaves of each tree. The flowers and bees clung together in their morning dance. Making the round she could see the sun triumphant in the sky. It shone warm and true against her bare skin. She kicked off her shoes to feel the warm earth meet the dew at her feet. She threw off her shorts and they lay like a discarded banana peel between the Pollack's house and Mrs. Granger's hedge. Her socks were the last to come off as she sprinted through Twin Oaks, as new and as bare as the day she was born, and finally ready to take her first steps back from the outland of enforced diminishment.

AGNES HAS HER CAKE

$\mathcal{A}$gnes had returned before the sun was directly overhead. She wanted to freshen up and change into a new suit—perhaps the dark blue with the pearl buttons or that lacy pant set in navy. It would be a shame if someone from the meeting wandered into the luncheon and saw her in the same dress and jacket she'd worn this morning. After all, it wasn't just the Twin Oaks Homeowners' Association, but groups from all over the county and even the state. Word had it that Edna Barrett, the head of the National Association of Planned Communities, would be dropping in for a surprise speech, and she'd be bringing her decorators with her. The ideas would be bubbling over, and she needed to catch every last opportunity. She had to make a good impression.

The Rutherfords had gone well this morning. They gawked at her designs as soon as she opened her portfolio. Nevertheless, she hated the way her stomach had rumbled halfway through the presentation. It was imperceptible to them, but it had shaken her all the same. It seemed that every time she built to a talking point on her list it let out a slow, tickling grumble as if to remind her who was really in charge of the day's proceedings.

"Forty-three points," she reminded as if dangling a carrot. She repeated it in her head as a bass line to the symphony that was her most brilliant pitch. They had eaten it up, as she knew they would. And though the meeting was successful, it had left her feeling empty and drained.

"Forty-three..." She balanced the Calliope's cake, large and unwieldy, on her knee, wiggling it onto the marble kitchen island. How she'd carried the heavy package this far was a miracle in itself driven by the need to impress. It smelled of promise and chocolate dipped in thick buttercream. The oaks reached up from under the cellophane. If she turned her head just so, she could make out the replica of her own home peeking out from the corner. With her nose pressed near the cool white box, she could pick apart fondant from pastillage, the different scents subtle but discernible.

She wondered how heavy Miss Cally had gone with her famous filling. The reviews called the dense fudge everything from heavenly to deadly. She scrolled now over the same comments she'd used to research the baker, finger hovering over one reviewer who'd called it "rich and sinful." Another boasted, "Too tempting!" She wondered if that was why they called it Devil's food. Was it too hard to resist? She slipped a nail between the slick waxed cardboard and the sticky cellophane tape fastening it shut. The tiny membrane popped with no effort at all. The lid fell back, as if of its own volition, and lay there still.

It was so beautiful. Blown sugar dew drops dotted the tiny branches of the miniature trees, no doubt formed from modeling chocolate. The smell was intoxicating. The houses stood sturdy and proud gleaming with a fresh coat of cocoa butter paint. Marshmallow, tempting marshmallow, placed a soft hand against her cheek with its sumptuous perfume. It came from the homes. They were cereal treats. She'd done her research. She knew. Hand piped flower beds and royal icing lawns dotted the landscape, each one as unique and as intricate as the next. She inspected, surveying every detail. She was slowly circling when she spotted it. In the back, just behind Mrs. MacMillan's house, where the Pollacks' lawn met the deep slope of the old woman's property, there was a tiny line, so fine it could be a hair. A hair! She couldn't have such a thing. A hair in the luncheon cake! It could be catastrophic.

Delicately, tenderly, without pressing or poking she ran her fingertip down over the edge. It wasn't a hair after all, but a soft seam where the fondant skirted out toward Mrs. MacMillan's lawn. With a gentle push she could lift a small flap for a quick glimpse beneath if she chose. She could just take a tiny look. A sound, a half moan, came from Agnes's lips as the rumble shook her insides. This was a need she knew too well. No one would ever know.

The skirt yielded easily and lifted all the way with her first touch. She gasped as it peeled upward, allowing full access to what was below. She stared, shocked but mesmerized. It was more beautiful than she could imagine, a strata of fudge and buttercream layered between moist layers of deep black cake. She eyed every crumb, every dollop of fluffy icing, and her mouth filled with longing and curiosity. She didn't push. She lightly caressed the layers from top to bottom, enjoying the texture and surface, each crevice and bump, the soft buoyancy of every wrinkle and the delicious pliancy of the filling beneath. It was almost unbearable. The shaking in her core came on so quickly that she could no longer resist. She slid her longest finger between the thickest layers, tentatively at first and then as far as she could go, wriggling until she found the treasure. Yes, the filling was there, unctuous and as tempting as any reviewer had ever gloated.

She sucked long and hard at the sticky fudge until her

entire middle finger disappeared into her mouth, emerging completely clean. For only a moment she debated whether to cover the cake back up, folding back the shift and tucking away what she'd done as if it hadn't occurred. But it was just too good. She thrust another two fingers into the fold, licking at the tips and padding at the soft crease where the skirt met all that heaven below. There were smears of crumb and chocolate on her lips that she licked at greedily, all the while digging tiny circles into the surface, pulling back more and more as her core roared its approval. It was so smooth and silky, the white buttercream on the top. She patted and tapped at it with her fingers, and once again licked them clean.

"Agnes, what on earth are you doing?"

She was hunched over the marble island, jacket crumpled in a heap at her sides, when the two women arrived. The ladies couldn't see with her back to them that she was licking her forearm from elbow to wrist to fingertip, or that she was covered in buttercream, chocolate finery and the remains of what was Mrs. MacMillan's backyard.

"Agnes!" she insisted tapping her foot as mothers do to children when they want them to move quickly. Annabelle spoke first, as usual. The fairer haired of the ladies looked as much like Agnes as her companion did. The three together could fill out a catalog advertisement for smart ladies' suits.

Abigail, the youngest, was more for action than words and had not given her friend time to finish. She had scurried into the kitchen and rounded to face the hunching woman.

"You really need to try this." Agnes was breathless and sluggish, euphoric. She pulled a line of buttercream from an untouched surface and spread it thick against her own cheek. It was so soft and silky against her skin. She rubbed it on her lips and face, and then again along the length of her neck.

Abigail took in Agnes' wide eyes, her plump chocolate lips as they drew on her covered fingers until there was nothing more. Her blouse was opened to the third button and her skin was flushed as she plunged a hand yet again between the layers, eyes closing in delight.

Whether Abigail knew it or not, a low groan escaped her as she watched Agnes shudder. Her lungs filled with a breath she held but did not let go.

Annabelle stepped toward the two, near the cake and unsure of what she was seeing. It was hard to breathe all of a sudden. Her face warmed, her temples throbbed.

"Agnes! The luncheon!"

Annabelle was the oldest of the three, though no one would ever have known it. Somewhere she had found the magic of youth, yet her eyes were wise with years and wide with what she saw. Had she looked at that moment in the mirror her skin would have matched her scarlet purse and matching pumps.

"What the hell are you doing?"

Abigail threw off her mint green blazer and placed her hands flat on an uncharted section of exposed cake, as a gypsy would a séance table. "Have you both lost your minds?" A bead of sweat ran down Annabelle's face. Abigail didn't notice. She tossed her full hair over her shoulders and without a word pushed face first beneath the crease. She licked at it, thrusting her tongue between the layers. She lapped and gulped between squeaks of joy and gasps for air.

Annabelle stood rigid, knuckles turning white where she clutched her purse, watching her companions in different degrees of ecstasy. Agnes was sliding her hands over the smooth cake top massaging the tiny hills and valleys of Twin Oaks. Animal grunts erupted steadily from the younger of the two. Her round mint bottom rose and dropped in time. Annabelle could feel it like a pulse inside her as she watched, transfixed. Abigail stayed bent at a perfect angle, hands still poised on the edge of the cake, her skirt still pristine. But her hair was wild. It fell in dark waves across her face dotted with flecks of white and smears of vanilla cream. She looked up at her stiff friend long enough to smack her lips together in approval.

Annabelle found it hard to get her breath. It caught in her throat in hot gasps. She peeled off the last of the suit jackets and added it to the pile crumpled on the floor. She was so close now. She could smell it.

"Are you just going to stand there and watch or are you going to come get some yourself?" Agnes thrust her hands into the surface she'd been smoothing, pulling up a supple round of cake in each and holding them slightly beneath her chin. She held them just as Annabelle tried to speak but couldn't make words, her face now dripping.

"Oooo... Mmmm..." was all the head of the Facades committee could say.

Agnes held out a mound to the lawns expert, who nuzzled it with her nose in a playful circle before nibbling at the top. Agnes flicked with her tongue and then bit hard into her mound. Annabelle felt woozy. She needed to take a big breath of air.

Instead she groaned low and long and fell to her knees right in front of the marble slab. When she lifted her face the others had joined her and were feeding her rounded mouthfuls by hand. She opened heartily, letting them cover her lips with icing, crumbs and thick globs of fudge. She sucked hungrily at Agnes' fingers, licking the length of her right palm. Abigail held her face in her hands while Agnes laid a heavy layer of lawn over the entirety of her silk blouse and up toward her face. It looked as though two green snakes had slinked up Annabelle's neck. The youngest ran a handful of fudge through Annabelle's fine hair, and she screamed with delight before falling exhausted in a heap next to the smart suit jackets.

The house was quiet then for all but the nurse and the man upstairs. The ladies basked below like satisfied cats, lapping until no crumb remained. There would be no mess when Adam returned. Not a soul would ever know what they had done.

MR. POLLACK'S ARMS

*"P*iggy-Pie, dinner!" He called down the stairs to the kid den, an entire netherworld dedicated to sprites, fairies and all things toy. And within seconds the chubby footsteps plodded in a shaky one-two until, smiling, Pigg replied at the door, "Tay, Dada."

"It smells good, Daddy. What is it?" As was the custom, Jack was flanked by the usual sous chefs as he stacked dinner rolls into a pretty pyramid on a large speckled dish.

"Macadamia crusted mahi-mahi with a mango salsa and mashed plantain." He sniffed, impressed. "Not too shabby."

"It looks like a rainbow." Mollie admired from so close that her breath steamed.

"Plantains are high in potassium, vitamin A and B6, much higher than a banana, and contain a significant percentage of dietary fiber for ease of bowel movement. Good choice, Dad."

"Thanks, Alton." He patted the boy on the head. "I

71

didn't think we'd get to our bowels until dinner started." He balanced platter and plate, holding a pitcher of lemonade in the crook of his arm as the children circled like bees toward the dining room.

April was waiting, back to the fray, fiddling with her final touches. Three lush plants looked as though they'd sprouted from the long lacquered table; a taller version of the three stood reaching from the occasional table. Candles brought a measure of warmth to the stark white room from the sides and above.

"April, are those real?"

She hadn't acknowledged anyone until then. She'd been admiring her newest find. "Yes, every one. It's a handcrafted chandelier. Those are real candles, not light bulbs. See how they match the ones on the credenza? I picked it up today, after the luncheon. Agnes says they're all the rage in her circles. Brings something to the room, right? Makes it look even bigger."

The kids buzzed with excitement. They were like that with change, and it didn't take much to impress them. Alton inspected the long stick matches as if they were an archeological find. Mollie made shadow puppets against her ivory seat cover. Pigg sang a nonsense song about stars while reaching for the booster seat underneath the chair. Good habits were developed, April said, and Pigg was a testament to her teachings. All the while Jack set out rolls and lemonade, and tiny dipping bowls for assorted sauces that ranged from mild to deadly; fragrant yellow pepper and pink sweet and sour. For the daring, there was a muddy brown hot sauce that came in a bottle marked with a grinning skull. He kept that one for April, who liked things hot lately, and by the looks of the bottle it would set her insides on fire. Plates clinked and the children chattered. April remained silent, tugging at seat covers and fluffing the drapes.

"You look nice, new outfit?" Jack popped the cork on a '93 and thought twice about his own glass before pouring

April's with the panache of a maître d. He settled napkins onto each of the children's laps before seating himself.

"What is that supposed to mean?"

He smoothed down his apron and inadvertently scratched at his arm. He regretted it at once. "Nothing...just that when you said you'd be getting changed, I thought you meant..." The words felt thick and sticky, like peanut butter in his mouth. "You look good."

She was weary. "I like to look nice, Jack. Would you prefer that I put on some sweats?"

He chuckled, though nothing about it was funny. Mollie laughed the way children do when they think they are supposed to. Alton arranged matchsticks into slender log constructions.

"No, April, I'd never suggest that."

"Hey Dad, did you know Mrs. Womack's dog is really smart?"

Mollie's serene blue eyes conveyed awareness beyond her years. She simply knew it was time for her to speak, to break the static between the two adults on either side of the table.

"Is that so?"

The girl beamed: "Gustav knows exactly what that little nugget is saying." She pointed at the toddler who was happily licking plantain from where it had dropped on the charger plate. "And no one understands Pigg..."

"Did you know that there's a scientist in Cambridge who says there's such a thing as telepathy between certain pets and longtime owners. And it increases exponentially the more time they spend together." Alton had forgotten his architecture as his eyes flickered in the candlelight. "Hey, do you think Mrs. Womack will let me follow her and Gus around for a few days? To study them?"

"Uh, I don't see why not." Jack smiled in spite of himself. "Kids, when I was nine, I'm pretty sure I couldn't spell phenomenon."

April smirked. "Alton, I think that is a fabulous idea.

Who knows the kinds of fascinating things you'll discover about the human mind. You may even find that that dog is smarter than his owner."

Jack inclined his head toward the children. "April, don't be like that."

Her voice was smooth. "Like what? It's nothing against that woman. I know plenty of animals that are far more intelligent than the humans they live with." She toasted, "It's a fact! Mollie, what are you doing? Don't play with your food."

The girl was decorating mounds of plantain with chunks of mango salsa. It was a large circle with what appeared to be two smaller pyramid shapes at the top that she'd brandished with tiny dots of cilantro and red pepper. She dipped her fork into the yellow sauce and splashed liberally, quite pleased with the result. She didn't slow when April spoke nor acknowledge she'd heard her mother at all.

"Mollie!"

She scrunched up her nose in concentration as she placed one last thin sliver of fruit at the center of the largest round before turning the plate for the table to see.

It was an orange cat, balancing what looked like a bird on top of its fruitful nose.

"Look, it's Paul..." She looked up for the word as if it hung on the new chandelier, "Clay spelled Klee."

Jack's face warmed with a full smile. It was a replica of what he wore on his arm, a warm mélange of color that popped right off the plate and into his heart.

"That's right, Mollie. That's actually very good. It looks like the *Cat and Bird*, doesn't it?" He lifted his sleeve and held his arm out under the light so the family could compare her work to the one he'd recently acquired.

The likeness was uncanny. Piggy squealed with delight.

"Yours may even look better. Your colors are much brighter." He winked, scooting off his chair and crouching beside Mollie's chair. Pigg tottled sideways to join him on the floor. "I'm still healing."

"Dada pretty cah-at-too." Pigg reached out to touch the kitty and bird on Jack's arm.

"A cat-too," Mollie giggled. At this even Alton smiled, taking pause from his match fortress to nod in agreement.

"Okay, put it away Jack." She looked at Mollie: "Eat your dinner now, Mollie."

He rolled down his sleeve and gave the girl a smile, flashing her the a-okay.

"You've got to admit, the kid's got talent."

"I have no doubt about it, Jack. All our children have been given great gifts. She reached out to the boy next to her and stroked his hair. Alton was engrossed in the crisscross pattern of his match house. "I'm sure Mollie is going to be an artist someday." She corrected, "A *real* artist."

If the Pollacks were a painting one might think they were praying right then. Jack's head dipped to his plate. April's naturally inclined to Alton's side. Mollie closely inspected three separate dipping bowls laid in front of her. All but Pigg looked reverent. The wee one chewed unabashedly, with openmouthed vigor. Tiny hot breaths filled the room like a silent bubble. It hung in the air just overhead until April broke it with a barb.

"If you ask me, what Mollie did is a hundred times better than that thing on your arm." Whether it was intended or not, April's eyes rolled candle to candle, from the chandelier all the way to the side table. "If you ask me, I'd say *that* doesn't even look like a cat."

Those flecks of yellow in her eyes, the one's he'd thought looked like the sun, were flame now, focused directly at Jack. Her face was calm and she spoke serenely, in the open house voice she used for walkthroughs of the neighborhood, the voice she used at wine tasting parties when he brought up the crazy woman next door. Her voice was warm honey, butter and biscuits, but poison seethed behind the words. It burned his skin and stabbed him in the chest.

"Say Jack, you're the expert. Whatever happened to art that actually looks like something? Did that go out of style?"

He rubbed at his arm again and took a deep breath. He scratched his whiskers looking for the right thing to say when Mollie beat him to it.

"May I please be excused?"

He loved that little girl.

April sat while he cleared the table. She rose only when he exited to the kitchen to blow out all the candles before they wept hot wax on the floor.

"You know, it was supposed to be a surprise. I thought you'd like it."

"A tattoo? Oh Jack, you must be high."

The words cut harder and deeper than any slip of a blade. His thumb stung where the knife caught, but he pretended neither had stunned him and kept his eyes focused on the sink. Breathing was important. He had learned to breathe through the present to forget the prodding past.

"I thought you liked cats," he said calmly.

She sniffed: "I like *my* cat, Jack."

"Right, you've had that thing longer than you've had me." He made a chuckle that sounded more like sodden wool than joy, but at least he was trying. "So it's like your world and my world, together."

He felt for a second like he knew what a statue must feel like with people walking past, looking but not noticing, talking about anything but what they saw right in front of them.

"Right Jack, nothing like sneaking off to your old haunts to show me how much you care."

The platter pulled at his hands as if it weighed one hundred pounds. He wanted to follow it under the soapy water and down into the sink, down into the pipes that travelled way under the house.

"I wasn't at my old... Do you really think?" The question hovered between the two of them like a toxic cloud. He tried to make things clear. "It's all upscale now. Restaurants, shopping, galleries." He wished she would believe him. "Everything's changed."

She stood so close he could smell the honeysuckle and yellow orchid on her skin, on tiptoe as she did years ago to kiss him on the cheek. But her lips had no intention to relive past affection.

"Did it feel good, Pollack, to have a needle in your arm again?"

He turned to face her, arms open in surrender. "It wasn't like that, April. I would never."

But she was stone, staring through him like a window.

"I can't do this anymore." He let the clean dish slide back into the murk. She stood as far away from him as she could while remaining in the same room. She was across the kitchen on the other side of the island, but she may as well have been on the moon.

"Then don't, Jack. No one's forcing you."

Piggy stood by the back gate smiling like a dimpled garden gnome. "Dada hoe-me?"

He scooped the cherub up in one motion, resting the child on his shoulder as if he were Bob Cratchett himself. It may have been July, but it might as well have been Christmas. He had cold shooting through him that he couldn't shake.

"Dada you strong."

He didn't feel that way. He arms felt like they'd turned to jelly, betraying him along with his backbone. He wasn't a liar, but he felt like one. Pigg stroked his face with a soft loving hand, and grinned wide. He basked in the innocent smile of one who only knew him as Dada, as Jack, the man he'd become, the Jack he wanted to be.

"Can-ee?"

Mollie and Alton came running on Piggy's cue. He handed each child, now circling, a lollipop as he did whenever they were all together in the yard. "Not in the house." They nodded in the bored unison that comes with reminders that need no reminding.

His temples pounded and his arm itched. It felt like it would tear off at the joint sometimes but that was in his head. He knew that. When his chest felt so heavy he couldn't breathe, there wasn't one physical reason for it. It wasn't asthma or smoking. It was nothing a doctor could cure, but it sure as hell made him sick.

The kids said he sounded like Tarzan when he screamed like this. It happened so often now that it had become expected. They licked at their candies and waited for the big one. But still he tried to provide cover. He played jazz and tribal drums at full blast. Now it was an old song from his grunge days, when his shadow was sexy, and his work wasn't a child's game.

It was reds and blacks today. They bled on the canvas like wounds. And when he stepped back touches of gold and yellows exploded to the surface. He kicked over a small can of brown and threw it at the corners like a caveman. It felt good to have disorder. The scattered newspapers and old sketches made him feel at home, his old home where he could be messy or loud, or not make sense. He lost himself there and was sweating by the time he'd had enough.

Then it caught him from the corner of the room. It caught him as was custom. Even from behind the cloth he knew those eyes were watching. They searched him. He felt childish feeling childish, but it was how he felt all the same, ashamed, like he'd been caught playing hooky. Oh, he was doing something wrong, and those eyes knew what he was doing. He pulled away the sheet apologetically from the painting he had started with passion, then ignored.

He stroked at the blank spots, hands like bricks. "I don't know where I'm supposed to go." The eyes hung like clouds in a placid sky.

The sun blushed its way into the early evening and he

inhaled deeply then counted slowly as he exhaled. He felt the tightness in his chest give way to the scent of moist grass. It was odd indeed how a one-minute conversation with a practical stranger could change so much. She had seemed kind and eager, glancing at his arm as if intoxicated by the colors that peeked out from underneath the sleeve of his white t-shirt. Her warm eyes had followed his every move, never narrowing, not even when he'd caught himself, embarrassed, scratching at that arm.

"Good night, Just Jack." She had looked over her shoulder and waved as she'd walked away.

STRINGS AND THE KEEPER

*"H*ey Strings."

"Thanks for coming, kid. Give me a hand over here."

Ben stood with his back to the door, a pen dangling from his lips. A tower of overstuffed cardboard boxes teetered short of falling at his feet. But he pressed his belly into the center, the lode bearing box pushing it like an elevator button back into the pillar, and the whole column once again stood tall. Adam stood by, like a gymnastics coach spotting the older man, holding his hands up high in case the whole project went south.

"I could have been here before nine, Strings. That would have been no problem. But I thought you wanted me here at nine."

The old man glanced at one of many cuckoo clocks and said, distracted, "Something came up. Now is just fine."

"So, what do you want gone?" He looked around the room that was divided seemingly into quadrants. One section was boxes. Another was for bags; garment bags, and grocery bags, canvas bags filled with party streamers, straw bags filled for island vacations and bags filled with other bags. There was the paper area, where lopsided stacks of magazines mingled like drunkards and eager piles of newspapers leaned in for a closer look.

"It's not that I want to see anything go." He took a sharp breath that caught somewhere in the back of his throat like a lie. "But for Bea, I've got to, I suppose. It's driving her crazy in here."

Bea kept a house the old-fashioned way. There were times she was on her hands and knees, negotiating the maze of Strings' odds and ends. Adam could smell the lemon oil on the clean wood floor.

He'd never thought of Ben as "old", but just then that was exactly how he looked, like a withered grandpa who'd forgotten his own story, and was lost in a train of thought.

"For Bea, then!" Adam reached into a crate filled with toys from another era. "How about these?" He held up a sad looking painted dog whose one eye had faded to nothing, its pull string worn to thread.

"No!" Mr. Chalmers said with a lunge for the box that made Adam flinch, but then composed himself with a step back. "I can fix that."

"You can fix a lot of things, Strings, but we're keeping this whole crate?"

It was loaded with the types of things for which secondhand stores were made. Tattered stuffed toys peeked out through the slats: monkeys and bears and lions; novelty mermaids, chipped blocks with rough edges, games with missing pieces and an agoraphobic jack-in-the-box that refused to pop no matter how much the music swelled.

Mr. Chalmers wasn't budging. "None of those go."

Three crockpots, a fondue set and an ancient pair of cast iron cooking tongs leaned against the far wall that Adam brightly thought of as the cooking corner.

"How about some of these?"

Ben leaned his face on his hands as if calculating some grand mathematical equation. "I guess one of the crockpots could go." The young man raised an eyebrow. "Oh, hell, and the tongs too."

The knock at the front door came as a surprise to at least one of the men. Mr. Chalmers tinkered with a cuckoo not yet ready to stop ticking. "Hey, could you get that Adam. Might be a delivery."

"Doesn't that kind of defeat the purpose? I thought you were stopping with the shopping networks."

"Oh, this isn't shopping networks. I got a box coming from an old buddy in Carolina."

The young man tugged on the heavy door.

Mr. Chalmers smiled: "Fireworks."

Adam was about to say something but swallowed the words like wine when he saw her at the door. She was beautiful in a berry shell, her tan arms extending as she reached to knock again. If there had been no screen between them, then their fingers would have touched.

In the confines of his most private place he swore he'd seen her one sunrise, a goddess flying through the night, her bare skin glistening like stars. His face felt hot as if it were happening right before him. But of course, it was a fantasy.

"Oh, hi Adam. Can I come in?"

He'd stood there stupidly, red faced, lingering at the threshold like a giant cobweb.

"Of course, Dawn. Nice to see you."

His voice cracked despite his effort to use the business voice, the mogul voice, the tone he used at board meetings and guest appearances at college computer classes. Instead he sounded like a paperboy collecting dollar bills for his route.

"Hey Ben, looks good in here. You moving out or something?"

"Clearing out some old things." He rubbed his chin, "For Bea, you know?"

Dawn knew Bea better than anyone. She knew, as well as he did, that it killed her to see things this way.

God bless that woman for her charms and her patience. He hated to see the sadness in her eyes, the look she tried to hide behind smiles and remarks about the weather when she came in from a walk down the street.

"Where are they?"

"Out back; I think Lucy's putting on one of her shows. Ponies today, I believe."

"She loves that horse, Ben...talks to it like it's real. Adam, did you see the horse that Ben fixed up for Lucy?"

He tried to think of a witty response. "Oh, yeah."

Her hair fell in thick silky ribbons across her face and halfway down her back. He'd never seen her wear it so free, not in real life. But in his dream, it flew behind her like a cape as she bounded down the street as perfect and pristine as the heavens.

"Thanks for keeping them this morning. I hate to ask you on such short notice. But you have no idea how long it's been since I've taken a nice, long shower. I was hoping you guys wouldn't mind."

"It's fine, Dawn. You can ask for an extra hour any time you like."

There was color in her cheeks. In Adam's too as he directed his gaze at Strings who had an unsurprising grin on his devilish face. "No harm in thinking about yourself once in a while."

"Thanks, Ben." She gave Mr. Chalmers a quick hug before inspecting the divided room. "Bea's going to love this." She took a side-step around a model carousel that skipped every third note before her eyes caught the young man's. "Nice seeing you again, Adam."

"Nice again too," he stammered, "seeing you, that is, is nice."

She gave a wave over her shoulder which Adam quickly reciprocated before returning his gaze to a tiny rider who over the years had come unglued. He drifted sidesaddle as the rest of his companions glided effortlessly to the shaky song. Adam was so focused that he hadn't seen Mrs. Ringhaus looking back through the sliding glass door.

"She likes you, you know."

"Huh?"

He was straining now to decipher the incomplete melody.

In days past they had called Ben Chalmers "Mr. Strings" because he was a master at improvisation, and songs played by ear. If an overzealous fan spilled a drink on a set list, no one would ever have known; he'd move through the show like clockwork, every soulful second filled with riffs he made up on the spot. Strings never missed a beat.

"She likes you, kid. Don't you see it? The way she looks at you? How you look at her? You're killing me. For some kind of computer whiz, you're a tad slow, no?"

As if waking from sleep, Adam looked at his friend with clear eyes. "Was this some kind of set-up, Strings?"

"It'd only be a set-up if it worked." He pulled a handful of magazines off one of the heaps and started leafing through them one by one. "Besides, it wasn't all for you."

"You're nuts old man."

"That may be true, but I'm right on you two. You should ask her to go to dinner."

Adam's face was doubtful. Strings clapped his hands together. "How about a walk together? That'd be nice. Baby steps, right?"

"Strings, I don't want to burst your bubble, but I can't just ask Mrs. Ringhaus out on a date."

"Dawn."

"Dawn..." He felt boyish and silly even saying her name. "I can't ask her out."

"Like hell you can't. You like her don't you?"

"Is it that obvious?"

"Kid, the last time I looked at a woman that way, I had no choice but to spend the rest of my life with her."

"Bea?"

He nodded. "Ain't no 'can't' when it's like that." Mr. Chalmers pulled up a stack of *Scientific Monthly* and sat beside him. "What are you so afraid of? What people will say?" The suggestion felt like bile in Mr. Chalmers' mouth.

Adam pictured himself walking arm in arm with Dawn, like the newlyweds down the street, catching lightning bugs with Lucy and Becca, Dawn tossing her hair back in the moonlight laughing as they frolicked together like a real family.

"I'm a lot younger than she is."

"Just a number," Strings shrugged. "There's eight years between Bea and me. Not to mention some of that other stuff." He sniffed and Adam smiled. "You think folks didn't have anything to say about us? Shit, her people wanted to have me beat to hell. Yankee cracker, sniffing around their little lady?" He whistled like a plane going down. "But I wasn't afraid. I was stupid in love with that girl."

"My mother would have a stroke. I can just see her at her next meeting trying to explain that to the ladies. They'd have a field day."

"Explain what? She don't have a thing to say to a goddam soul. Kid, no one can tell you your own business. And that's the truth. You spark with who you spark with, and no one in the world can tell you otherwise. Of course people want to try. I say, let 'em talk with their fancy hats and looking down their noses. No offense to your mom, kid."

Strings shoulders eased. They'd both joked often about the association ladies. But you never knew with family. It was a touchy thing. He sighed. "You're the one who's got to live with the regret, not them. So, if they want to talk, let them talk 'til they run out of steam. They always do, you know." As convincing as his argument was, the young man did not look his way. "No one can tell you how to live, son." His voice lowered and his eyes lost most of their impish gleam. "The day you start thinkin' they can is the day you start dyin'."

Adam never talked like this with the man at home, the one on the third floor. He wished he hadn't thought of him then. "So, you think she really likes me."

"I wouldn't be hounding you if I thought she *liked* you, kid."

Two knocks came like a loud heartbeat that pulled Mr. Chalmers up from his seat so quickly he looked like a marionette.

"They're here!" He skip-stepped puckishly to the door and was greeted by a hulk in a russet delivery uniform who spoke in a voice far higher than Adam would've imagined.

"I need a signature, Mr. Chalmers. And initial here."

The older man was humming with excitement.

"Are you having some kind of party or something?"

"Something like that."

The box was as tall as a fourth grader and as wide as a fridge, and behind it the hulk was wheeling in three more thick, stubby boxes stacked on top of each other. By the way the dolly leaned, they looked heavy.

"What are these?"

Ben was already elbow-deep in the largest one, pulling out colorful packages marked with rainbows and laser beams set against a dark sky. He muttered to himself as if reciting a strange incantation: "Pyro-Spyro, Jumpin' Jimmy, Midnight Streakers, Wicked-Devils. Hot damn!"

"Strings, what do you need all this for?" He couldn't recall a party Mr. Chalmers attended or threw, nor a yard-sale, social, or neighborhood meeting of any kind. But this box overflowed with strange explosives fit for a city-wide celebration.

"I don't." The old man leaned so that half his body disappeared behind the cardboard flaps. He pulled out package after package from the seemingly endless contents then pulled himself upright, straw strewn over his t-shirt, smiling like a scarecrow. "A friend of mine in South

Carolina's got a store room full of these things. Full of them! He asked if I could take these off his hands. Take them, he says. I didn't even pay shipping." He added, before diving back inside the box, "Something that good comes your way, you don't pass it up." Strings' muffled voice came from a thousand miles away. "I suppose I'll keep them around 'til they're collectible. Folks go nuts for stuff like that on the Bid-Bay. I can corner the market on out-of-stock firecrackers."

"What about all this other stuff, Strings?"

Adam felt foolish talking to the old man's rear end. He crooked his neck to look down the hall to the back of the house and for a second caught the view outside. Lucy galloped in a tiny loop around her mother. The sun caught Dawn's hair so it rippled like dark water in the sun. But as soon as she'd surfaced she'd disappeared out of the window frame, bringing him back abruptly to the task at hand.

"Decision time, Strings." He gently kicked at a basket of hairdryers. But he'd lost the old man down the dark hole. "Strings, the boxes? I've got to come back with something."

His friend emerged triumphant, with an oversized peppermint stick in his hand. But it wasn't candy, on closer inspection. It was far too thick and at least a foot and a half tall. On the bottom was a stout blue cone that was only vaguely familiar until Ben turned it upright.

"Is that a rocket?" It looked like something straight out of the comics, cartoon-large in Ben's hands.

"One-night Special—The Big One! They only made these for a few seasons, years and years ago. I'm talkin' way back. They used to call it the Showstopper, because the sucker lights up the whole damn sky. Sounds like a bomb when it goes off." He turned it slowly in his hands, admiring the bygone craftsmanship. "This one's the keeper, kid. Not letting her get away."

From around the house Dawn surfaced, shrinking

down the street with her girls close behind. Adam felt the corners of his lips rising slowly to the swell of the carousel.

"You can take all those things against the wall there. I'll pack up some of these for a rainy day," he said picking with his free hand through sparklers and roman candles. "And that other stuff piled out front, I'll bring it out to the garage. *Out of sight like*." A note of amusement colored his words. He was now talking to the young man's back. "I'll do what I can to keep the peace."

Dawn disappeared from view. Outside the neighborhood was stirring. Mrs. Granger's silver sedan slunk up the cul-de-sac like a molten river. She'd be wondering what goods could be pilfered from the eyesores that blighted the Chalmers' property. Mrs. Womack puttered by with her golden companion, absorbed in conversation. There were signs on the trees for yard sales, and garden parties for the selected few. They waved in the warm breeze like butterfly wings.

Adam turned to his friend, who was again admiring his cartoon explosive.

"What do you suppose you do with something like that in a place like this?"

The old man smiled. "Blow it up."

THE FAT LADY SINGS

As the rest of world slumbered in darkness, he'd crept to the shed as if sleepwalking and painted well into the night. Whenever the work called him like a siren, it seemed as if there was no gravity, or time, and the simple downward strokes became a meditation as his vision appeared upon the canvas.

Tonight it was her arms, warm and golden as if they'd seen a hundred summer days. He'd seen those arms so often, pumping like pistons, propelling her around the cul-de-sac on those mornings when he went out for his paper. Her arms were long and lean but in no way delicate. They would never droop under the strain of everyday toil and tension. She never seemed to flinch while running through the neighborhood; she always looked straight ahead. What that must feel like, he couldn't guess. Those arms suggested strength beneath the surface that now seemed impossible to replicate with his brush. But every man was born with certain limitations, and he'd left her before the first rays of morning light.

In fact, April had beaten him to the sunrise. She was up and in the shower long before he rolled out of bed, smug and unaware that he'd only just returned. With any luck Mollie and Alton had slept uncharacteristically late. And when Piggy finally got to asking for breakfast it wasn't for the usual pancakes or toast.

"Can I have steak, Daddy?" Of course when Pigg said it, it sounded more like, *C'igh haff take Dada?*

Jack scratched his head the way a father does when he's buying time. There was some filet mignon in the freezer. If he crushed some cornflakes, it would be like cereal was somehow involved. He could reduce down some orange juice and whip it into a dipping sauce. The possibilities were brewing. It was unprecedented that Pigg had asked for something that wasn't candy, so Jack scrambled for the better part of his early morning preparing chicken fried steak nuggets for his youngest child. But all the while she haunted his thoughts like a reminder.

April breezed through the kitchen with the express purpose of kissing him on the cheek before heading out. Nothing passed between them but the slightest smile. And when Mollie and Alton came downstairs, they weren't noisy, but seemed to be conspiring with each other over summer secrets. Something was in the air.

After breakfast, he found himself tracing over his own strokes as he wiped up the milk ring that Pigg had left behind. There was no lagging chatter in the kitchen, just Jack and his thoughts in the vacant room, every one of them amplified in the silence.

It was so hard to leave her unfinished, dangling in the dark. Again, he thought of her arms. They were so encompassing, as if they could keep the day itself in place. He envisioned those arms moving mountains, enwrapping themselves around the earth and holding up the world if the sky were to let it go. It was hard to replicate strength like that, but this morning he needed to try.

He always felt strange in the front yard, like a zoo

animal on display. He was self-conscious picking up his paper or pulling in garbage cans. He was not the type to drink coffee on the porch or make small talk with the neighbors about fireflies or zoning changes. Why did people feel the constant need to discuss the weather? Could they not confirm the heat, the sun or the rain, for themselves? It was stupid to state the obvious. Mrs. Granger would look over the lawn and make a passing remark that his bluegrass was green, and he'd find himself wondering if she was taking some kind of shot. It was hard to tell with a statement so unnecessary. And it didn't help that she was always smirking with those long teeth over some undisclosed joke that perhaps she and April shared.

He associated most of his run-ins with the ladies about town with a general feeling of unease, a rolling burn in his belly. It would catch at the back of his throat when he smiled or told stories, coloring his face pink as he spoke of home improvement stores or garden club functions. The only time it dissipated was the night of the Chardonnay, when the words flowed like liquid gold from his lips and April had watched with an openmouthed stare.

He hadn't expected her to be standing there as he made his way back to the shed. His was an innocent gesture to finish what he'd started during the night, but in an instant he'd felt as if he'd been found out. She was standing in her front yard, not disembodied on his two dimensional canvas, but in the flesh, ripe and warm in the sun. Of course the eyes were different than those in the painting. Hers were green or gray, and not icy at all. But the arms were right; lean and dazzling. She stretched them wide to the sky as she watered her plants. It was as if she knew what he'd been up to back there in the shed and she was showing off for reference.

He felt caught, as childish as it seemed, like a peeper staring through a window. Her hair was down and flowing, her running shorts traded in for a slim berry shell. It clung and glistened, showing off the length of her tan arms, so much like the painting. But these were different somehow, pliant and alive. He'd never seen her like this, whistling every so often and crouching down to check on each fragile bloom. She dug her hands into loose earth, tucking roots safely back into place.

"Dada canee?"

He was interrupted by the chubby hand, sweat-sticky on his wrist.

"Piggy, it's not even ten o'clock." Somewhere in their invisible agreement, that was designated as the suitable time. But the child didn't scamper away to return a few minutes later for another try, as Jack would've guessed. Pigg stood there watching with Jack as the stream of water at the other house crossed through a swath of morning sun. It was beautiful, arcing up toward the clouds, drops of water dancing down like delicate jewels.

"You see da rainbow Dada?" Pigg's face was ninety percent cheeks with a smile that could melt polar ice.

"Yeah, I do, Pigg," he said, and without a thought placed small, wrapped taffy into the child's chubby hand. "Here. But your brother and sister have to wait."

When she saw the pair looking over, she probably assumed the colored spectacle drew their stares. From the distance she couldn't see his face had flushed crimson as he ducked his chin into his chest like a turtle gone scared.

"Where are those two anyway?"

The answer came from the back of Pigg's head as the child scurried into the yard.

"We go to da moon!"

He lifted his hand over his shoulder without looking, duplicating his child's move exactly as he waved to the neighbor, never once lifting his eyes. *Creep.*

It's not that he coveted her. It wasn't like that. But he wanted his heart to stop pounding and his face to stop sweating. A throbbing in his temple boomed in his ears. It matched the steps approaching on the walkway. Yes, his rising breath sounded just like the rhythmic exhales of the overheated genius dog. The woman grinned at Jack. He'd done it again, hadn't he? He must look like a psychopath standing here deep breathing on the lawn. *Just Jack*, he'd told her to call him, like he was some kind of midlife weirdo popping finger guns at young chicks and winking from his front steps. Christ, he felt like an idiot.

She had always been the one who smiled at him so easily, with no sidelong glances or downturned eye. Surely he'd blown it. She'd always seemed so kind, with her easy voice and accepting heart. Now she looked at him with one raised eyebrow, as if she'd smelled something foul.

He wanted to say hello but turned back to the house without a hint of a wave. The damage couldn't be undone.

April came in like a hurricane only moments later.

"Did you see what that woman was doing outside?" This was her amused voice. It was loud and confident, full of lilt and emphasis on syllables that normally merited less attention.

Still, Jack felt strangely disarmed from the whole morning, and off balance. His lady was still waiting, unfinished.

She didn't give him a chance to answer. Either that or she'd grown impatient with waiting. She was about to be funny after all. "She was hand feeding him a bottle of water...and then she got down on all fours and was washing off his paws." She added with emphasis, "On her knees," and waited for him to get it, until that was no longer fun, "right in front of our house."

Jack held his blank look.

"She was on the ground, Jack."

He failed to see what was so strange.

"The whole neighborhood could see."

As shocking as that seemed to April, it didn't register as worth a second thought to her husband. It made it no less funny to her just the same.

"How do you suppose she's going to get up?" It wasn't often that April giggled, but this had tickled her in a way he hadn't seen in years. "Don't you think that's funny?" She tipped her head upward, as if expecting someone to sing along to a familiar tune. That seemed more shocking to Jack than the image of Wilma Womack crawling on the ground outside his house.

"Not really."

Her mirth had a funny way of shifting to frustration.

"Oh, please, you'd laugh if you saw that fat woman wobbling around on the ground. Don't try to take the high road, Jackso—"

"JACK."

Her smoky eyes widened so they looked in reality as aware and awake as the makeup attempted to make them appear.

"Excuse me."

"You heard me, April. Enough with the Jackson Pollack. Enough! And no, I wouldn't think that was funny, okay? Wilma Womack is a nice enough lady."

April's eyebrow remained raised. "Mr. High and Mighty!"

"She never says anything about anyone. The lady minds her own business. Give her a break. She's harmless." A slightly amused look crossed April's face. "You don't have to be cruel."

"I suppose you're right, Jackso—Jack," she corrected. "I shouldn't make fun. It's a shame, really. It's just that she should really do something with herself."

Jack could sense the old April coming back, humor drifting from her voice as she shifted into business as usual.

"Like that running woman. You know the one I'm talking about, don't you Jack?"

His stomach lurched and he felt boyish, like he'd been driving a bumper car that crashed unexpectedly.

"Huh?"

"That Ringhaus woman, Jack—the one that runs... She was watering outside a little while ago and you were looking right at her. Just now, *out front*. Don't you remember, dear?"

April wasn't one for sweethearts or dears, but he played along.

"Oh, that one, yeah. You know me with the neighbors." He attempted a smile but his lips were too dry and stuck to his teeth in a snarl.

"Shewas a mess, and her husband took off. But then she did something with herself." She mused, "I suppose he did her a favor. That's what the Womack woman needs."

"A favor?"

She raised her eyebrows triumphantly, smirking like a cartoon cat. "Jack, that woman was so fat. And a complete shut-in only a few years ago."

"I don't even remember her living here a few years ago."

"Of course you wouldn't," she smirked. "Who would? That's my point. Now she's made something of herself and she's worth a look, isn't she?"

There was a tense energy behind her smile, not the selling houses spark that fired her up for closings, but a strange tautness like violin strings about to snap.

"April what are you getting at?"

She poured a glass of murky green juice from a bottle with a handwritten label and took a long gulp. "Are you happy Jack?"

"April, it's not like that."

"Are you happy?" She accentuated the words as if they were warring countries, giving them lots of room to breathe, or to battle.

Happy seemed to be a strange galaxy. He lived somewhere in it, between not entirely miserable and it could be worse.

She wiped a strand of shining hair from her forehead, her face calm as she slid the curtain to peek at the prize roses out back.

The words wanted to come out, words of content and

satisfaction, but she was so superior in her crisp suit, even now looking so serene, even without the army of scowling suits that usually followed wherever she went.

"Are you?"

"Am I happy?" She scoffed. "Of course I am."

He felt like he was sleepwalking again, images flooding his mind like ice: her hard shoulders when he tried to kiss her goodnight, her turning away from the children's hugs because they would mess up her expensive conditioning treatments or new nails. It made him shudder. She was a world away from the tender girl that had sat cross-legged as he painted.

"I don't think you know what that means."

"And your friend out there, the Pillsbury dough girl? She does?"

"Is that what this is about? You're always telling me I should talk to the neighbors."

"The ones that matter..."

With such venom she responded, and he scarcely recognized her voice. "Don't be so cold."

She slammed down her bottle so hard that he feared it would shatter in the sink. "I could be happy..."

"But you're not." The statement stung in his throat, though they'd both known the answer long before either had spoken. What hurt more was what he knew he was about to say. "Is this over?"

It was a wide open feeling putting three words out that could change everything he knew about his own existence. It was a chasm to eternity kind of question that left him feeling infinitely small and unsure of his own footing.

"What a silly question." She laughed. "You think I'm some kind of quitter all of the sudden? I thought you of all people would know I don't give up on anything, *Jackson Pollack*. A failed marriage? Yeah, right. So I can be like them? I don't think so. That would make you happy, wouldn't it?"

His uncertain sadness was matched if not surpassed by

her growing anger.

"It is far from over. It's not over until I say it's over." She was breathing heavily. "Until the..." she snapped her fingers, "...cows come home. Oh, I can't remember the stupid saying, but it's far from over."

He didn't dare finish it for her.

If April was good at anything, it was selling appearance. This evening she had her game face on, and for anyone not in the know, it was dinner as usual. Once the dishes were cleared and the children were off playing, he made his way to the shed. But his new friend was just in front of the gate, this time not on hands and knees. She stood upright, genius dog at her side like a footman.

Her heart shaped face was framed by a crown of soft chestnut hair. Her cheeks, so much like Pigg's, erupted in dimples at the faintest sign of a smile.

"You made off like a bandit before I could say hello earlier."

"Hello, Wilma, nice to see you." He didn't feel the rumble or the burn, simply the peaceful breeze against his skin. It was soothing on his arms.

"Glorious day today. And a more beautiful night even, don't you think?"

She gave the golden a squeeze, and when she smiled it seemed as if she had the answers to the earth's deepest secrets.

He hadn't felt strange talking about the weather. During the brief conversation he hadn't thought once about disappearing to his shed, or the ethereal eyes, or even the arms he'd left waiting. Once he did get back to painting it had only taken a few strokes to finish what he'd started. One highlight and he felt complete.

He was whistling when he finished, a few notes of the tune he'd heard Wilma singing as she'd walked away.

BABY STEPS

*"M*ore tea?"

"No thank you, Mrs. Granger," said John Harbage as he looked somewhat helplessly at his wife, took her hand in his, squeezed it, and then checked her pulse. "But this is some wonderful spread, right Daphne?"

The low table was set with golden chargers filled with scones and berries, tiny flowered bowls of assorted creams and butters and a crystal platter piled with treats and savory delights. Daphne touched none of it—not that she was impolite, but naturally quiet and shifting between smiles directed at her hostess and fellow guests.

"This marmalade is killer," John complimented. "Honestly, I've never had anything like it."

"That's because I make it myself, John. Everything is homemade."

He found himself nodding dumbly as his cheeks grew warm. This was going to take some getting used to.

"Even the fruit," said a woman in a suit that looked just like Mrs. Granger's. She chimed proudly, "I grow everything out back. I have my own greenhouse."

Mrs. Granger was surely the star of a strange chorus line, while the other women flanked her in a definite pecking order. There was the nervous one on the far end, the one that liked growing things and looked younger than Daphne with the same girlish build. But she looked like a string bean. And if she was a bean, the lady next to her was a tomato. Her suit clung in places the others did not, and hung in ways that defied gravity. The women on the other side of their hostess looked like a sunny sky. April, the lady who'd found them the house, wore yellow, yet again. And the one beside her, their new neighbor, wore sea blue. All sat side by side upon the white tufted couch, from smallest to tallest at the center, so symmetrical, like a rainbow gone sharp. Mrs. Granger was the point.

"We at the association like to make everyone in Twin Oaks feel welcome."

"It's so nice having such a young couple in the neighborhood," the green one gushed. "What are you, like twelve?"

"What?"

"You must forgive Abigail."

Abigail straightened her back and sat tall, adjusting herself at once. The tight look that briefly crossed Mrs. Granger's face melted with the butter on her black currant scone. "You two look like you can't be much older than twenty."

He cleared his throat uncomfortably. They got that a lot, mostly because it was true. If someone had told him a year ago that he'd be walking hand in hand with his wife through some high-end, cookie cutter development, he'd have hit them in the head with his skateboard. Then again, if he knew anything by now, it was that life was full of surprises.

"Abigail is a bit of a joker." She smiled at both of them but at Daphne in particular. "What she means is it would be so nice to have someone like you in our organization, so young, some new blood, so to speak. We do hope you will consider joining us down the line."

Her teeth were so bright, her cool white hair pulled taut. For an older woman Mrs. Granger's skin was smooth and unlined. There was not a wrinkle around her mouth or anywhere on her suit, giving it all the look of polished steel.

"We're always looking for members," said the one in red.

Daphne's eyes shifted from John to the window, then to the women in front of her.

"It's definitely something she'd consider, right Daph?"

She nodded while taking a gulp of tea, her bare knees knocking together in a nervous bounce.

"Hey, I know. Why don't you all tell Daphne all about the garden club? She's got a hell of a thumb for that stuff. Sorry. Heck. Ladies, where are my manners?"

April gave a reassuring wink but any intent to speak was cut off by the tomato.

"Don't worry, hon. I don't see anybody blushing."

Daphne's hands relaxed, so they no longer looked white at the knuckles where she'd been gripping the cup.

"Do you ladies mind if I excuse myself for a minute? Could you tell me where the—"

Before he'd gotten the words out, the one in red blotted her lips and bounced to his side as if her legs were on springs. "I'll show him. Don't worry yourselves, okay? You, sweetie, make yourself comfortable. Let the ladies take care of you. We won't be but a minute." She smiled over her shoulder as she ushered him down the hall. Her hands were tiny but left their mark on him, like hot little irons on his skin.

He could hear Abigail starting up a conversation with Daphne, and crossed his mental fingers.

"What does that say on your t-shirt?"

He heard the muffled sounds of Daphne's first words all day. "Obey. Do you have any coffee?"

"She's cute," the woman said barely over a whisper while shimmying close enough as they made their way down the hall that their bodies appeared to share a seam. "Your wife," she urged when he didn't answer.

Along his right side he could feel the lingering heat where their bodies had touched. She felt feverish, but wasn't flushed or sweating. Nonetheless, he swore he could feel her heartbeat throbbing against him. It must have been in his head. His nerves were shot.

"And you, you're just a pleasure, aren't you? I'm so sorry about Abigail. If she made you feel uncomfortable... Some of us have better control...over our mouths."

"I'll be right back, Mrs.—" No one had mentioned her name.

"Annabelle." She smiled coyly. "And it's *Miss*." She watched as he closed the door. "Don't worry, sugar. I'll be waiting when you're ready."

He dialed the phone as soon as the door divided them, grateful for the quiet that the closed door provided. Dr. Stein answered halfway through the first ring.

"Hey, it's me, Echo. Yes. Better today, I think. I got her out of the house like you said. Baby steps, right doc? I think we may be out of the woods. Sure, of course. No, we came down the street. I wouldn't dream of it. Okay, you have a good day too."

It was a small victory, but he'd take it. A breakfast with the local ladies club wasn't his first choice, but he'd eat dinner with Satan himself if it meant getting his Daphne back.

"That didn't take long at all."

The young man looked as though ten years had been lifted from his brow. He smiled crookedly, distracted as he crossed the threshold.

She was leaning up against the wall with her jacket slung over her shoulder like a fifties starlet. She had the look down: pale hair pulled up into impossible waves, lips lacquered like plump fruits.

"I just needed to wash my hands. That marmalade..." He smiled while holding them up, clean.

"Mrs. Granger's got her secret recipe. It *is* delicious." She had him by the arm to lead him back to the other ladies. "Mouth-watering, really..." Her steps were slower on the way back, more determined. She inhaled deeply as if catching a scent. "Irresistible..." She chose there to stop investigating something that had fallen into the well cushioned crease beside her heart.

"Listen, John, you're a very nice fellow, and I for one am happy to have you in the neighborhood."

"Echo."

"What's that?"

"All my friends call me Echo."

She turned to face him without questioning the name. "Well then, Mr. Echo," she paused, so her point would be clear, "you want to fool around a little?"

"I'm sorry?"

She leaned in playfully and shimmied so her tight waist and full hips beat against him, like knocks on a door. On tiptoes she pressed her lips so close, the words were burning kisses. "*La petite mort?*"

He stared at her, confounded, and not because he'd failed French. Surely, his past had done irreparable damage. He was hearing things now.

"I promise you won't regret it."

Unsure smile on his lips, he began to speak certain that this was some sort of initiation, a joke meant to be shared with the others, some good natured new neighbor hazing.

The suburbs were like that, weren't they?

She put a hand on his chest and again he felt the heat flow from her fingers.

"No one will ever know." Her hand felt like it was burning through him. "Come on." She pulled it away, thoughtful, tracing her upper lip with a fingertip. "Or if you like, you could put me to work. I'd be happy to oblige." Her hand went roaming.

"Be a sport; give me some of that young hot co—"

"Stop that!" He grabbed her hand and held it in the air. "What are you doing?"

She had a wild look in her eyes. "I'll never tell." She called after him as he flew down the hall. "No one keeps a secret like me."

The others were in a full blown discussion about diatomaceous earth when he'd come flying into the room like a madman.

"Daphne, get your purse, we're getting out of here. Sorry, Mrs. Granger, we have to go."

"Is everything all right, John?" Mrs. Granger asked as calmly as a grandmother would ease a worried child, but the others exchanged anxious looks.

"Something's come up. So nice to meet you, ladies."

"Echo, what the hell was that all about? I was *having a conversation*."

"Believe me, it was time to go."

"You wake me up. You make me get dressed. You walk me all the way down here..." she looked like she was doing an equation "...and then you suddenly want to leave?" Her eyes were clear and focused in a way that didn't frighten him. "But I'm the crazy one?"

He fought hard to contain a smile. "It was just time, okay Daphne?" He squeezed her hand, tight. "We'll try something else tomorrow. Baby steps, right?"

Her brow furrowed.

"For me," he adjusted. "I'm still getting used to all this." He flipped his hand out at what was in front of them. A woman watered her front lawn while the dad next door patted a small child on the head. From a distance, the chubby woman down the street leashed up her golden retriever for their daily walk.

"This is like a whole other world. I need time to take this all in." He tried to make it as light as he could. He didn't want to lose her again. "Look at that. There's a butterfly, for God's sake, in real life. And I bet you five bucks that bird is about to start singing." He nudged her shoulder with his head.

"Hey, you did great today."

"I did."

They walked in rhythm together, like partners in a three legged race, listening to their steps until the bird proved that Echo could be right about something.

"I'm not a baby."

"I know you're not." He breathed deeply, thankful for most of the morning's events and hoping that the best was yet to come, when for the second time this morning he thought he'd been hearing things.

Daphne was laughing.

"I did better than you did." Her face was so beautiful when it was relaxed.

"Yeah, you did."

"Not so sure I'm ready for a ladies club. But I liked Abigail. She's all right. And April, of course, and Agnes and..." she was ticking off ideas on her fingers again "...Annabelle."

Annabelle had pressed her hot mouth against his flesh and his body had responded in spite of his shock and his reticence. For a second he'd wanted her so badly he'd ached. His conscience grew restless with the thought of it.

But he'd known that he loved Daphne the day he met her, even though they were, by all standards, still children. She was gentle and caring, of course, but from the start it had seemed like she had insights about him that no one could have had; it was like she read his mind.

"It could have gone a lot worse," she shrugged.

"Yes, I guess it could have," he acknowledged.

She smiled and guilt burrowed through him like a parasite.

IT'S TIME

"Hello, anyone here?" Dawn poked her head inside the door expecting Ben. It wasn't often she needed to knock.

"He's out in the garage, honey." Bea's face looked as though the sun itself were hidden just behind her eyes, her smile brightening as she spoke. "Doing some work."

In the hours since this morning the house had changed. The clunky pots were gone and she could see the thick tassels of a fancy throw rug where a fat mountain of old magazines had lived for as long as she'd been coming here.

"It's amazing."

"Isn't it though?"

Dawn had expected a challenge balancing the plastic containers with the overstuffed paper bags, but a hopscotch path through the front room had been cleared.

"Where's the mess, Bea?" The voice behind her was frank and adult despite the incongruous nature of its sound.

"Lucy!" Dawn's voice dropped an octave, thick with admonition.

The child merely shrugged behind a large jug of ice tea. It sloshed as she teetered into the room like a penguin.

"That's all right," Bea chuckled, relieving the girl of her load. "It's gone—most of it, anyhow. Benny's trying to clean up in here for me." She pushed a box of beads with her foot and put a hand on her hip in disbelief. Then, as if she suddenly remembered something she'd forgotten, she called into the kitchen, "Where's my Becca?"

"Oh, she's coming," said Dawn. "She's got a surprise for you. But I'm sworn to secrecy."

Bea rested the cool jug on her shoulder like a sleeping baby. With the other hand she led Lucy to the kitchen. If either hand had been free, then she would have held it to her face in shock when she saw what waited in the kitchen with Dawn.

"What is all this?"

"I thought I'd bring a late lunch," she answered not looking up from the task at hand. She had the farmhouse table filled end to end with plates and bowls of all sizes. Sliced cheeses and salads nestled between plates of fried chicken and fresh rolls. Spreads and dips, condiments in convenient mini-cups and platters of crunchy sliced vegetables made a rainbow on the periphery.

"Lunch? Honey, this is a feast. It's only us two, dear."

The words caught Dawn off guard. "I know. I just wanted to do something nice for you." She stared at a napkin she'd folded into neat fours. "Felt like a special occasion or something today. I don't know. Like we should be celebrating..." She fiddled with a toothpick that wouldn't sit straight. "You both do so much for me. It's the least I can do."

Bea scanned the table and found a stack of finger sandwiches that she hadn't previously noticed. Dawn looked out the window, though Becca had come in through the front door.

"Thought you might be looking for your friend..."

Dawn pushed a piece of hair behind her ear and found

a piece of celery that had fallen out of line. "My friend?" But her query was hollow and her face went a shade or two deeper. "Is he still here?" She spoke in a hushed tone, and her little girl smiled.

"Mommy likes Adam."

"Lucy!"

"What? You do!" The girl shrugged as Bea put her arm around her. "You do that thing with your hair when he's here." She glanced up at Bea. "She never does that."

Becca had come in and was clearing space for the large covered dish she placed at the center of the table. "Do what? That thing with her hair?" Dawn's gasp was hardly subtle. "Mom likes Adam."

"Becca!"

"You do," she insisted. "She does!" She turned to Bea with the staid look of an attorney pleading a landmark case. "*We* like Adam, too. Bea, can you make her talk to him, please? It's time already."

Bea didn't know which was harder to believe, the banquet on the table, or the frantic nature of the way Dawn had been straightening out the cutlery. Dawn wouldn't flinch if a plane crashed into the house, but she was rattled this morning, absolutely distressed.

"Girls, why don't you go out to the garage and see if Benny needs some help? I'll bet he's got some real treasures out there that you might walk away with if you're lucky."

Lucy was jiggling the door handle at the first mention of treasure, but her older sister stood by the table, pensive and a bit protective.

"Okay, but don't touch. This lid stays put." She nudged the heavy plate in the center of the table. "It's a surprise."

"You have my word."

"No peeking," she cautioned before disappearing through the door.

Bea chuckled before the hinges clicked in place. "You're going to have your hands full with that one."

"I already do." Dawn's eyes lifted from the table and brought the tension with them, at least momentarily. "She's got a mind of her own."

"That's not a bad thing. It's good. No one's going to ever be able to tell her what to do or who she needs to be." Bea's lips caught on her teeth, which Dawn mistook for thirst. She was back at the table filling a tall glass with sliced lemon and mint, unaware that her friend was biting hard on her lip to fight back a thought that had taken her unexpectedly.

"She's so smart...too smart sometimes..." She handed Bea the glass. It looked like it had come from a magazine at the supermarket checkout.

"So pretty, it's almost a shame to drink it." She smiled, more thankful for Dawn than Dawn knew. She took a long slow drink and relief washed over her. "Delicious!"

"They are right."

Bea sighed knowingly but didn't say anything. She leaned against a chair and watched Dawn with her head inclined. She drank the tea and admired the handiwork laid out before her.

"I thought he might still be here," she conceded. "But that's not why I brought lunch. I really wanted to thank you, and I can't remember the last time I had a morning all to myself."

Bea dipped a carrot stick into an herbed spread and bit into it with a crunch. Her eyebrows raised in approval. "All this looks like it could go on one of those brochures that they stick in our doors every summer." She feigned a familiar starchy voice: "Twin Oaks at its finest!"

"It does, doesn't it? Who knew I had it in me?" She was embarrassed suddenly at the extravagance. How absurd a feast for so few! "I guess I did go a bit overboard. I'm like that when I'm nervous." Her voice descended. "Everything has to be perfect."

"What are you worried about, Dawn?"

Whether Dawn knew it or not, she was pawing at her

forehead like she was smoothing a wayward bed sheet. "Bea, I could be his *mother.*"

"Come on... When was the last time you saw a seven-year-old give birth?"

"Okay fine. But what if he laughs? He could laugh. It's ridiculous, isn't it?"

"I have eyes, and that boy's got wings."

Dawn felt like she needed to clean the table. She felt like she wanted her calendar back. And she knew by the three creases under her fingers that she was scowling.

"Real love can put fangs on a bunny, or make a grown man cry like a baby. The real thing can make an elephant as graceful as a butterfly." She clucked her lips, amused by more than the dip, "A little romantic, I know, but..."

Dawn jumped at the sound behind her. "What did I say about slamming doors?"

"Sorry, Mom." Becca shrugged as Lucy darted to her mom and threw her arms around her.

"What's wrong?"

The little one rubbed her face against her side. "Benny yelled at me."

Dawn's eyes travelled from Lucy to Bea, and then rested on the older girl.

"It's true; he kind of snapped at her. He told us to leave him alone."

Benny looked at those girls like they were twin sunrises on a midnight wasteland. But by the looks on their faces, neither of the girls was telling tales.

"I just wanted the doggie..." Lucy sounded like she was singing an old country song, holding on to each syllable before letting it go.

Bea's shoulders slumped and she brushed the girl's hair away from her eyes.

"The one in a beat-up wooden box... It had a fuzzy monkey with it, and a lamp that won't light?"

Lucy nodded, her head glued to her shoulder, her arms wrapped around her mother's waist.

"Benny gets real particular about some of those old things. They sometimes get him in a bad mood." She put a finger under Lucy's chin. "Every once in a while he loses his manners. But he thinks the world of you both, don't ever doubt it."

"Why don't we bring all this outside?" Bea eyed the symmetrical stacks of bowls and plates with a raised brow. "Like a fancy picnic," Dawn added, and before she'd finished the girls were stacking sandwich plates on top of lidded bowls.

Bea lagged behind hoping Dawn would catch the hint.

"I'm sorry, Dawn. You know he doesn't mean anything by it. He gets like that with that box. I don't know why he keeps it." The younger woman held up a hand to swipe away any further explanation, but Bea ignored it. "No, it's not okay. He's got no right to make those girls feel bad." There was a hiccup in her words, like a skipped record, as if she'd lost her train of thought. But Dawn knew better.

"Benny's got this big hole that he can't seem to fill up, no matter how hard he tries. No matter what he builds or buys or stacks in my sitting room, it's still there." Her face, though troubled, showed not one line of worry. "It makes him mean sometimes; edgy, keeps him up at night. I try to help him as much as I can but..."

Dawn stood in the doorway, Bea at her side, both looking out on the yard. Until now she'd only seen the differences, but even with the many years between them, they were more alike than she'd ever assumed.

The girls laid out a sheet that Bea hadn't used for years, but it was still as pretty as she'd remembered it, blue checks that popped against the green lawn. The colors were bold in the sunshine, as if they'd been brought back to life after a long respite in darkness. To Bea, the little girls looked like tiny fairies as they placed dishes into each square like perfect puzzle pieces. Any hurt or pain had been put aside now. This was better than any picture in a dusty old magazine.

"I'm going to talk to him," Dawn said.

"Oh, honey, you don't have to—"

Bea motioned back from where they had come, but Dawn wasn't talking about the garage. "It's time," she said.

MRS. GRANGER AND THE VAPORS

*"T*here must be some sort of misunderstanding."

"How is that?" Annabelle looked confused if not miffed.

"I'm not taking visitors."

Annabelle stood, bottle in hand, leaning toward the door as if she could will it to open. But Mrs. Granger didn't budge. The association president stood like a giant stone in the doorframe.

"Close your mouth, Annabelle. You look like a fish."

Annabelle tried on all accounts to seem unfazed, resting a hand on her hip instead of scratching her head in confusion. The Granger house was always set for a party or picnic. It was the place where the tea flowed continuously and the flowers never wilted, where tiny finger sandwiches seemed to replenish themselves on spotless china plates. But more than any of that, it was a place for respite and sanctum for the weary, as long as they were in the association. At any given time a lady could seek out Mrs. Granger for everything from decorating advice to stock tips. The most embarrassing of boudoir questions were known to share the floor with tenet reviews of basic etiquette. All was fair in the sitting room of the president's grand home.

Mrs. Granger didn't take phone calls. She took visitors in her sitting room.

"Whatever it is you want, Annabelle, you can call April Pollack." Everyday vulgarities like telephone calls were deferred to the vice. She should know that by now.

"I've brought what you wanted." Annabelle lifted it much as a child would in an attempt to impress another, and far too quickly. The brownish liquid sloshed inside the bottle as her hand jerked up toward the closed screen door.

"I can see that," said the white haired woman, not a line breaking the porcelain of her smooth face. "And I will take that, appreciatively." The door cracked enough to let Mrs. Granger's hand slip out and extract the bottle.

"I thought maybe we could sit down for tea?"

"That won't be necessary," she smiled coldly. "Not today."

Annabelle shifted from one foot to the other, a sad look of befuddlement clouding her face like a mud mask.

"Is there something wrong, Mrs. Granger?" Her teeth were white against her red lips and though the smile was as broad as her cheeks would allow, it was all emptiness underneath and both ladies knew it.

Mrs. Granger's smile was thin but held a world of secrets. She opened the screen door wide, but not to allow her guest to come inside. She stepped out onto the porch so she could speak more plainly.

"I know it must be difficult for you to contain your urges, Annabelle, but you need to learn to control yourself." She spoke as a mother might instruct a young girl with a needle and thread. "You can't just take what you want like some kind of barbarian. You need to work for it. There are rules, you know."

Annabelle nodded dutifully. This was not a shocking statement. The sentiment could be written on a banner somewhere so that every member of the association could see it at meetings for as much as it was shared. Still she inclined her head as if the information was novel, although what was said next almost knocked her off the step. Mrs. Granger caught her eyes in her steely gaze though the thin smile never wavered.

"That boy is not for you, Annabelle. He is Daphne's husband." Annabelle's eyes widened and she tried to mask her terror by brushing a hair from her face. The effect made her look comical, like a faltering clown pulling faces for the crowd. "And she's not ours yet..."

Annabelle clawed at her throat as if she could scratch her voice free. But Mrs. Granger was giving no ground. "There are ways that we do things, Annabelle. And there are ways we do *not* do things. You know that. There are consequences for our actions." All the while Mrs. Granger, with the poise of a dignitary, backed her down the stairs and onto the entry path. "Now, I don't want to *hear* any more about it."

The two women marched in a strange tango toward Mrs. Granger's gate, the president leading the woman in red as she took giant steps backward away from the stately home. When she left the picket gate her hand dropped peacefully to her side and she stood staring serenely at the woman in front of her with undivided attention. Even so, the president leaned in and spoke barely above a whisper, the words more sinister than any secret and all too familiar to the woman in red.

"*La petite mort?*"

"How...did...you?" She grabbed for the words, stupidly. The ladies had been rooms away. But that never mattered with Mrs. Granger. She knew everything that happened in that house; it lived and breathed with her as if they were one creature.

Mrs. Granger's thin smile melted as if everything

behind it had been wiped clean, her voice no longer soft but practical: "Annabelle, you're a *lady*." She shut the gate between them and over the sharp points that divided them, reminded one last time, "You need to remember that." She stood at the gate to see Annabelle off in the right direction, and before she was too far away she remembered her manners. "And thanks for this..." She brandished the bottle with a brochure smile.

In the old days she might have gilded it a bit more, put on about having her vapors or not feeling up for a visit. But times had changed. Annabelle had made that clear. Nevertheless, she had what she wanted, gripped tightly in her hand, and that was all that mattered this afternoon.

Back inside the house she took stock of her kitchen, immaculate almost to the point of absurdity. Her countertops gleamed like glass and her cabinets looked like they'd never been touched by human hands. A gathering steam filled the air with a bygone smell, syrupy and bittersweet. It stung as she inhaled, but she craved the burn. Spicy anise and coriander mingled with lemon. Abigail's herbs filled her head like opium, and she drifted in the scent feeling like her twenties had never faded.

She flicked the cap off Annabelle's decanter and plunked three sluggish drops of the thick brown syrup into the mixture. She watched them disappear like the past. Breathing deeply she waited for the sound she knew would come. The notes nuzzled her earlobes like secrets. Gaining confidence they scratched against the silence until they filled the room.

Entranced, she stirred the pot counterclockwise, and with a tilt of her head let loose the white shift of hair that fell like a sheet against her shoulders. The scent was deep inside her now, and the steam grew so dense that it was difficult to say where her hair ended and the fog began. She waved her hands like a conductor, and though her eyes were closed, she saw something that made the light of the kitchen seem dull and plain.

The voice was elegant and unwavering. It was not the voice heard at meetings, definitely not Mrs. Granger's voice. This was a smooth, velvet voice that could soothe a crying child or make love appear from nowhere.

We'll meet again, don't know where. Don't know when. But I know we'll meet again, some sunny day.

Had her eyes been open she would have seen the pot glowing, brighter and brighter with the heat of the moment and the swell of the music. She reached into the haze to pull something still intangible toward her body. It was warm on her skin; she could feel it turn to weight against her palms.

"It's not nice to keep a lady waiting." A new voice, as fresh as honeysuckle from the vine.

She opened her eyes and she was no longer Mrs. Granger but that long-gone girl with the blazing auburn hair. And he was there with her, so handsome, so dark and as sensuous as the day she'd met him. His thick full lips parted in greeting but as always could not form words that she could hear. She could make out a faint shape as he spoke her name.

Her mind told her that she was in her kitchen, dancing with a phantom, but her heart told her that they were together, heart against heart. She could feel his skin again against hers and see it like India ink against paper. Once he had called her his porcelain doll, and it wasn't a lie. She'd be his until the day she died, and thereafter if she had her way. The phantom lips moved to speak again but she held a finger against them to stifle the attempt.

She pulled him by the waist across the dance floor. He was finally here with her, after all this time. He was in the flesh as sure as she was standing...in her pristine kitchen.

She ran her hand across his cheek, and he mouthed something she could not make out. The mist was returning now, and no matter how much she rubbed and clawed at her eyes his image was fading. He was gone in seconds, her hair fading to white along with the receding image of his face.

Mrs. Granger pulled her hair back into a tight, compact bun and whistled while pouring a tall drink from a decanter that she kept tucked away.

It was the kind of day for dreams, wasn't it? Yes, today dreams were written across the blue, blue sky. She killed the heat under the pot on the stove and ladled out a heaping dose of marmalade for the gin waiting in the icy glass.

She took one last look at her neighborhood before pulling the shades and drinking it down.

CHOCOLATE

"*T*a-da!" Becca lifted the cover with a ceremonious flourish. "Surprise, I made it for you!"

Bea clapped her hands together once and held them under her chin. "It's beautiful, Becca."

The girl stood a bit taller. "Mom did the oven stuff. I *am* a kid, remember?"

"Of course you are." Bea winked admiring the intricacies, each embossed detail pushing through the shining glaze. She didn't have to affect approval as adults often do. It looked like it had come from the fancy pastry shop downtown.

"It's your favorite, isn't it?"

"Root beer cake? Baby, you don't even have to ask.

Bea had made this cake for the girls on special occasions, but none as special as today.

"Tastes like fudge." It was a secret passed down from her great-aunt to her mother, and then down to Bea. "But how did you...?"

"We've been testing some recipes." Dawn put her arm

around Becca's shoulder.

"From the Internet," the girl added.

Bea couldn't help but sigh like a happy dog with his favorite toy. Dawn and the girls looked like they should be on a shelf at the store, in one of those pictures that comes with the frame. And the sun was shining without a worry in the world, like it had never heard of a cloudy day.

"Amazing how times change." She knelt down on the blanket. "This came to me in a whisper in my kitchen. Now you can look it up on your phone." She picked up the serving knife. "It's almost a shame to cut into it. You even got the fancy pan—the one with the flowers, like mine."

"It *is* yours," Lucy said excitedly. "Benny helped us."

She sliced into the cake and served slices to the girls who stood like patient saints before taking a bite. They were waiting for Bea. "Mmm, this is my favorite."

The little girls followed suit. Dawn also dove in, a look of relish on her face, having recently given up on her spreadsheets and forced deprivations.

"I love this icing."

"Glaze," Becca corrected.

"I love how you got the filling so true to the original recipe," Bea added.

"I love how it's chocolate," Lucy munched. "Like Bea."

"Lucy!" Dawn's face exploded into red blotches and she had a hard time not spitting crumbs across the blanket, reacting mid-chew.

The girl's eyes brimmed with tears that had been threatening to appear for some time. "But she is..."

Dawn moved to take her aside as she did when she was about to correct her, but Bea leaned close to Lucy placing a protective arm in front of her.

"But I am; it's a fact!" She held up the arm that held the plate, looking at the cake and then at her own dark arms. They ate in the uncomfortable quiet that follows a scolding. Bea, when Dawn was occupied, made silly faces

119

holding her forkfuls up next to her forehead, to her elbow and to her knee.

"She didn't mean anything by it, honey." Bea threw a balled-up piece of napkin at Dawn then kissed the little girl on the head. "She's not like that."

The tears bubbled down Lucy's cheeks despite the smile that grew on her face. She looked at her hand. "I look like the plastic cheese." She looked at her mom for agreement. "The kind mom won't buy in the store."

Dawn inclined her head in agreement. The blotches were fading but more prominent than comfort would allow.

"Mom looks like strawberry cake," she giggled.

The statement was as plain to see as the sun hanging overhead and it burned a large crack into the icy mask Dawn had worn only minutes before. Lucy was dry and giggling by the time they finished. She scurried off with her sister to play as her mother and Bea cleared the dishes.

"Guess he's not going to join us after all," Bea sighed. "I was hoping he'd at least come out to say hello." She folded the blanket carefully. When the breeze was right she could still smell traces of the old detergent, the one with a drawing of the ocean on the box. "I wanted him to see how good simple things can be."

Dawn waddled, penguin-like, hands full with leftovers and folded paper napkins. "I made him a plate." She lifted a tin dish with a flat white cover like a trophy and followed after her friend. But Bea wasn't looking. She was quiet as they walking back into the house then settled at the big empty table.

"How odd that one little change can affect how you look at an entire place..." Looking down the hallway it was clear that the sitting room had changed for the better. Even the wall in front of Bea was as bare as a white movie screen. But Bea watched as if a movie were playing.

"It looks amazing, doesn't it?" Dawn breezed behind her, leaving the plate for Benny on a side board. "You never know what somebody's capable of when the time is right." Dawn was preoccupied with tidying. Had she not been absorbed with her tasks, she would have seen that Bea's sentiment had not matched her own.

"No, I suppose you don't after all."

Bea had the hum of the refrigerator and an occasional drip from the sink to keep her company after Dawn had given up. She didn't say that that was her intention as she scoured the tabletops and folded linens but it was implied in every look toward the closed door, in every stolen glance at the room he'd started to make new. Whether she said it or not, the wait for Benny to emerge had gotten the best of her. After an hour, Bea had had enough.

She stood with her face so close to the door that she could smell pine oil and the faintest touch of old suppers still clinging to the wood like castaways. It was strange here all of the sudden, as if a breeze had snuck underneath the doorframe. The cool metal went icy under her grip. Her blood pressure was sometimes so low that everything felt cold. But this was a different kind of chill, one that dropped like a wrecking ball into the pit of her stomach. She couldn't hear him in there.

"Benny?" She knocked at a door in her own home. How strange to do that, but she felt that she ought to out of respect for the task he'd undertaken. It wasn't easy for him to dig through these old things, and worse to unload them after all this time. There was no light inside except for stray rays that filtered in from outside and bounced off the heavy beams in odd shadows, but she didn't trip as she stepped down as she assumed she would. No sign of clutter or junkyard debris blocked her way to the light switch. All of it had been piled into two giant stacks that blocked the view behind them.

"Ben?" Her voice had an odd quality, not quite an echo but that tinny reverb sound made by two tin cans on either end of a string. It was an empty room sound.

Bea was still as light on her feet as the day she'd turned

nineteen. Even so, it was hard in the dark for her to navigate the piles that seemed to balance so precariously. She took her time and didn't raise her voice higher than a murmur.

"Ben, you must be hungry. Come in now."

Her foot caught against the cornerstone of the far pile, the entire mountain shifting with the tired sigh of times gone by, and Bea almost cried out until she saw what the small box contained. His smile was infectious, beaming out of the frame like pure sunshine, and at once Bea felt the warmth of a tear running down her cheek.

"Ben, it's time."

There were so many piles back here, many smaller than the first two but prolific enough to make a labyrinth out of a once large open space. Garbage bags and bric-a-brac, antiques and cardboard boxes stood like sentries by the door. Nothing about any of this was disconcerting. In fact, it should have given her a feeling of satisfaction that Benny was finally coming through on an old promise. Yet none of this was sitting well.

The old wobbly ladder lay ahead. Like a compass needle, it split the rooms into hemispheres. It loomed in front of her like a distant nightmare. She'd never climbed to the top; it was just too high. She didn't want to look.

At first she'd thought he was on tiptoes. His face was serene despite the surroundings, like no worry could trouble him anymore.

"Ben!"

The old man shuttered, startled and then embarrassed.

"Bea, I wasn't going to..."

The rope was tied as perfectly as any seafaring knot. It swung like a pendulum in front of the large round window.

Bea never raised her voice, unless she was singing in church. And she was never one for cursing. But there were some days that were worth exception, and today was one. "Just what in the hell do you think you are doing?"

Benny spoke over his shoulder but didn't turn from the

noose. He did not let it go or look away.

Bea's tear returned, bringing friends, families and lovers with it. "Why? How could you do this? How could you do this today?"

"You weren't supposed to see..." He held her hands tightly now in love and fury, frustration and woe. "I just wanted to see..." Her eyes met his. "I just thought that if I could see it his way, then maybe I could make sense of it, why he went through with it." His eyes drifted to the spot that marked finality. "I just wanted to see what he saw."

"Oh Benny, it wasn't about what he saw *then*, it was about what he saw his whole *life*. He went too gently through this world. And it ate him up." She swallowed hard to subdue a sob. "That's all."

Next to the ladder was the sad looking dog with the wonky eye, the tattered pull string and brown velvet ears. "He loved Chocolate, didn't he?" The words cut through Bea like lightning and she bolted upright, eyes focused on her husband. Remarkably, she smiled.

"And science... He loved trying to see how things worked. He just wanted to fit."

Benny held his wife's hands and he could see himself in her damp eyes. They were so like his, still waiting for the missing piece to fill up the big empty. And then he said it out loud, what had lain dormant like the dusty old box he hid away in the attic: "David."

MR. HARBAGE'S HOPES

"I think I like it here."

Daphne toweled her hair dry at the foot of the bed. He wasn't much for hopes but lately it seemed like his wife had come back.

"I'm glad, Daph. Really, you have no idea."

"Abigail wants to come over with some clippings to start my plot, heirloom herbs I've never even heard of. Do you think?" Her nose crinkled in a familiar way that made Echo remember a simpler time.

A year ago this neighborhood would have been hell, a nightmare place where roots grew from his toes and he was buried alive. Now it seemed like Shangri-la.

"Thank you for doing this for me." She crawled up the bed like a cat and sat next to him where he lay. He could feel her silk robe against his leg as it fell to the floor. "All of it."

The past weeks seemed like a lifetime ago. One good day could do that. One good day had the power to erase the scars that the bad days brought with them.

"Of course."

It's not like it was a choice for Echo, but instinct to survive. He couldn't live without her, and seeing her suffer was more unbearable than any estate planning seminar he'd ever have to attend in this new future. The days of silence were so hard. Each day was the same, frantic calls to the doctor; hours spent trying to break through. She sat catatonic and he'd speak soothingly.

"Daphne, you're my butterfly." *A year ago he would have laughed at this.* "All those caterpillars are happy enough, but then something happens, right? That's all. Something just happens. They hide away in that warm cocoon, but they're so much better when they come out." He'd wanted to hold her hands then, but instead he'd lean in as close as he could so their eyes were a mirrored pair. "That's you, Daph, my butterfly. Bad things, scary things happen. But you're through it. You've made it."

He wanted to hold her close, to smooth back her hair. Instead he spoke in a soothing rhythm. "Think of all those little caterpillars that never get to come out. They're still hiding away, and they don't even know there's a sky above them. Daphne?"

Half the time he felt like a fool. But he missed the lilt of her voice and the light in her smile. A year ago, they might jet to Belgium for breakfast. Now he was giddy that she'd simply walked down the street for tea. How things change.

She was so beautiful now with the moonlight behind her, her smooth skin bare and radiant. Though he knew better, he reached out to stroke the delicate small of her back. She drew away with a shudder, her voice accusing. "No." Then she lay down beside him, stretched long on top of the sheets. "Can't this be enough for now?"

He swallowed hard and responded, as always, in stride, "Of course. I'll be waiting when you're ready." The words staggered him like a punch. They seemed warm in his mouth, like caramel. And he'd heard them before.

I'll be waiting when you're ready.

He shook the thought out like a cobweb, clearing his head for the task at hand. The nightly wind- down took concentration and the patience of a saint. He'd never thought of himself as the kind that could quiet the mind and simply wait. But he'd do that for her. He'd walk through fire for Daphne. If he wasn't careful, that's what it felt like sometimes, a fire building from within, lying awake next to the stark naked beauty beside him. She never climbed in under the sheets. She lay like a corpse, skin glistening in the darkness, night after night as he lay idly by. Not a caress or a kiss passed between them. Sometimes she would turn her head and look into his eyes, or hum a sad tune as her lids grew heavy and she drifted off. He stroked the pillow above her head but never her hair. The slightest touch could set her off, and she'd be up all night. Instead he traced the line where the pillowcase met the bed, watching her until her breathing slowed and he knew she was off somewhere in a world that would never hurt her.

Patience was proving difficult tonight because somewhere in her smile he thought he saw a light. Could this be the night his Daphne broke through? He wasn't looking for romance novels or a b-grade skin flick, but admittedly today had held the promise that the girl he missed might return for good.

"You okay, babe?" He whispered but she was already on her way out, belly rising and falling in slow time. Her stomach was flat and muscular, like the rest of her. She was far stronger than she appeared in the daylight in her oversized t-shirt and cut-off shorts.

Her chest rose and fell like a peaceful sea. He loved her by the ocean, and on the mountain lake, once on the side of a river on a kayak trip. God, he missed her so much. He had to let his mind go. He couldn't get up and walk away. She'd feel the shift in weight on the bed and that might set her off. It was hot in here. Daphne's body responded when the air-conditioner kicked on. He had to look away. It was torture. At first he tried to see it objectively, as if looking at art. But the hurt and desire outweighed the aesthetic and it was too much for him to take. He had to make his mind go blank.

He washed his mind like a blackboard seeing only the backs of his own eyelids. But then the sparks came through.

Annabelle's body was so hot against him in that hallway. She was thirty at least, an experienced woman for sure, with large, firm breasts and a thick round ass, her waist cinched tight like a bowtie. She smelled like honey and something he couldn't place, perfumed like cardamom he'd smelled on the islands. She wasn't really his type, his type being Daphne, but there was undeniably something about that woman... God, did she want him? He had felt her heat from across the room.

He slid off the bed without upsetting the sheets and stumbled to the bathroom. He didn't click on the light; afraid he couldn't finish what he'd started if he did. He closed his eyes and found what he needed in the dark.

She was fourteen when they went on their first date, fifteen when they fumbled in the backseat of his best friend's car. She didn't know what she was doing, but Daphne wasn't afraid of anything. He liked her daring. He thought of their trip to Bali for Spring Break a few years back, the cruise that her parents brought them on to Greece, suntan oil on the private deck. He let the warm memory glide over him as he tried to stay quiet.

Whether it was nerves or shame he seemed stuck in a holding pattern, so close to where he needed to be but not getting where he wanted to go. It was like that dream he'd had where he stood on the edge of the high dive but could never jump. He needed a friendly push. Annabelle helped. She straddled him on Mrs. Granger's hallway floor. Her legs like cobras squeezing the life from his body. He expelled a guilty breath and Daphne's face returned.

It was easier to think now. The house was quiet and he knew she was sleeping soundly. It was safe here.

Two weeks ago they were packing up the old apartment, not that old, or apartment, were accurate descriptions. Being a rich kid had its advantages, and for a while he'd been naÃ¯ve enough to assume that the rich never had cause to worry. But everyone has nightmares.

They were packing up electronics in bubble wrap; in his heart he'd hoped this move would be it. She was so distant, so far away, that turned-off look clouding her once sparkling eyes. Her hair was matted to her head and she often muttered to herself. The naive part of him that secretly made wishes hoped she was going over packing lists for the big day.

"What's that, babe?"

Her head snapped up.

"The filth is everywhere. Thieves, perverts, whores, hookers!" She ticked them off one by one. The tears behind her words filled her blank eyes. "They're everywhere, Echo."

He breathed deeply and crossed his arms over his shoulders before speaking again. "We're going to get away from all this, Daphne. Start fresh." He searched her dark eyes for a single spark of recognition. "It's going to be okay."

In his head he kept a tally of the quiet days because they ultimately lead to chaos, like an ominous roller coaster building to a giant death drop. The silent days sent an icy chill through his core, but in his heart he feared the disquiet even more. And the lead-up was torture. When it finally came, it came quickly, because it had been hiding in the silence all along. Their first week in the new house proved to be no exception. And Twin Oaks welcomed the bedlam with open arms.

She huned in the main entryway that first night in the house, moving boxes on either side of her. In any other world the after dinner sight of his wife bent over in panties and camisole would have sent him to a very happy place, but Echo's insides turned to ice.

"Arthrup, Joseph Engle, 63, stroke, leaves behind wife, six grandkids. Bostwick, Rochelle, 39." She gasped. "Meyer, Jeremy, 7. Seven, Echo, Seven!"

He bent to pick her up and she jerked her hands away, leaning for another paper, finger following down the columns, tick, ticking in that familiar fashion.

"Lawyer, baker, unemployed. She liked to sing." She whipped around and searched one of the boxes until she emerged with the crumpled pages of a coffee shop magazine. "This girl filmed herself throwing puppies into a river. *Puppies*. This man fed his *newborn baby* to a dog." Her head bobbed side to side as if it couldn't stop. "No one safe."

"Daphne..."

"Today's a bad day for dying, John."

He repeated her name, this time pleading with her. But she looked at him with eyes of broken glass.

"It's a bad day for dying."

The quiet had returned after that, descending like nightfall as she folded in on herself. But this morning had undone all of that, like magic. The walks, the talks, maybe it was the fresh air like Dr. Stein had said. Whatever it was, the new neighborhood seemed to have worked its spell. And for the first time in a long time, Echo was happy.

She was exactly as he'd left her, not a wrinkle on the sheet where she'd slept like an angel. He watched her until his eyes couldn't stay open any longer and it was hard to tell reality from the dream.

Echo hated to, but he was hoping.

JACK'S SPACE

*S*ometimes he thought her eyes looked startled; at other times accusing or hurt. Above all, they seemed to glow with awareness, taking in the surroundings like two search lights. It was often too difficult to guess without context, no way to determine if their passion was joy or hatred. Whatever quality they seemed to convey at a given viewing, they always looked straight through him. Today the surprise seemed clear to both. She was almost finished. Then he would leave her.

He'd leapt from bed this morning a man with a cause and without a worry wasted on whether or not he shook the frame as he sprung from the sheets. It was no matter now anyway. April practically slept in another time zone. She was tucked away safely on the far corner of the bed, not a pillow laid amiss, Solomon curled beside her. Neither noticed he'd gone. He remembered when they'd huddled together on a shabby twin, limbs tied together like play strings. Now she couldn't even call it a bed: it was the *Western Monarch, the largest bed available in the continental United*

States. Her voice rattled his bones when it took the tone of saleswoman. It came out at family dinners and on the way to the movies. It was a foreign voice that belonged to someone Jack no longer knew. God, he hated that bed.

But that was hours ago. And April had grudgingly given in to breakfast duty at Jack's prodding. It made up for the missed tuck-ins and nights spent wining and dining. He knew it had less to do with guilt and more to do with space. The more time he spent out here, the less he spent in there, and whether she admitted it or not, he knew his wife had become grateful for the time spent alone.

With a delicate hand he shaped the curve of her cheek. It was supple and full with the slight blush that sees the world as a new and inviting place. It colored the rest of her now, softening the lines of her arms, lifting the burden from those troubled eyes.

How she'd changed during their time together.

His stomach roared angrily reminding he'd not yet eaten or had a break for hours, but they were so close now to the end now and there was so much at stake.

"Da-daaaa!" Pigg ran full speed hopping into Jack's arms in a leap of trust.

"What are you up to, little one?" He couldn't help but smile. Pigg wore a funnel like a hat and a cardboard box cut into pieces and painted silver like a sandwich board.

"I'm a aleen," said the child through an uneven toothy grin.

"An alien, that's great." He raised an eyebrow warily. "Wait, are you friendly?"

Pigg's response was a sticky kiss and an arm around Jack's neck. "Wanna be a asher-not?"

He forgot the lady who waited. Their time would come soon enough and there were only so many summers left for aliens and astronauts to exist together peacefully. Mollie and Alton had joined them. A set of dark blue sheets from the upstairs linen closet was cradled in the girl's arms. Alton dragged a set of folding chairs, like a lame horse, through the garden. And both wore a look of wonder and inspiration that practically ignited the second they saw their father waiting for them. Together they built space right there in the front yard.

He was being a cyborg when Mrs. Ringhaus ran by, if he could call it that. She looked nothing like before. Her hair was half up and half down, and instead of staring straight ahead as she often did, the woman seemed to look around at the neighborhood, at the trees and at her surroundings. Her fevered pace had broken, and for the first time he saw her smile.

"Good morning!" She raised her arm on impulse to check a watch that was no longer there and then called back over her shoulder, "Let's go, let's go. Keep up, slowpokes." The mini caravan emerged behind her, two young girls on bicycles. The bike with the streamers was ridden by the younger sister and teetered on its training wheels. The older girl's eyes widened as her mouth dropped open and she called out to Alton, "Nice space fort!"

His son beamed at her immediate recognition. "We're astronauts," he called back, adding in qualification as they passed by, "amateur, that is."

It wasn't quite noon and already he felt like a lifetime had passed. There was glitter in his beard and glue on his hands but none of it mattered. Beams of light filtered through the tiny holes above and they twinkled like wishing stars. He couldn't remember feeling at ease here ever, but now he moved through the flaps of their minute universe without a second guess. He lay in the grass looking into the cosmos while thinking about nothing, not himself, nor her, just the tiny glitter stars and the peace that comes from space.

The footsteps came like meteors before the light came crashing in.

"What do you think you're doing?" She tore the sheet off in one hand, her eyes burning like cold fire: "My sheets!" Not a hair on her head moved though the sheet flapped in the air falling on her like a toga. Her hand remained clenched at her shoulder.

Jack lay with hands behind his head like a lazy river fisherman. "We're in space."

April's nostrils flared as she breathed all too rapidly.

"Space?" She spat the word like poison through clenched teeth. The children stood like statues afraid of impending annihilation. "Mollie! Alton! Go inside! Take Pigg!"

They were gone before all her words hung in the air together. April stood over Jack, sheet clutched in one hand, her eyes wide and intense. And he lay there like Huck Finn, a wrinkle of a grin breaking his serene face.

"Up!" she commanded.

"I'm not a child, April." He almost chuckled.

She kneeled down so that their faces were closer than they'd been in years. "Then prove it."

Her movements became a flurry of rage in dark blue, and when she whisked into the house he wasn't sure if he should follow behind. But he did. In that he snapped up like a robot, in one automatic movement that held no thought of what was to come. It was predetermined by then, an answer that had been buried within him long before he ever had lain upon that warm summer grass.

"April, we don't even use these." His voice was calm and even, serene like untouched water, no ripple in sight or far beneath the surface. "It's been years."

She, on the other hand, was less of a mystery, smooth on the outside, perfect as usual. But up close, what lay beneath those eyes was as ragged as an old security blanket gone through the wash too many times, one tattered and frayed at the edges.

"That's not the point." It didn't matter how long it had been since either of them had felt any of the 1,500 threads against their skin. "They're Luxor." Her eyes didn't blink. They accused with alacrity and defiance, neither of which he understood in the least.

"What is that supposed to mean?" His voice was stronger than he intended, like an old boom box with the bass turned up all the way.

She stood motionless, but he was right. It only strengthened him more. The final word came out with a schoolboy chuckle, clarifying his view on the matter in case any was needed. And then, like an afterthought or a death blow, he added at last, "It's not a big deal."

Both of them knew the gravity of these words as the darkness descended between them. Her voice lacked the volume that his carried naturally, but the depth was there.

"It's a very big deal." Both knew that these were Luxor sheets in Nile Cerulean, a shade unavailable in the United States, and that it had taken a few conference calls and at least three favors to have them flown in from the Azure coast. "Do you have any idea how much these cost?"

"What the hell does it matter if they don't fit the goddamn bed?" There was that snort again, like the kid in detention who laughs when the teacher's back is turned. Only he wasn't hiding, and April was looking right through him.

The Luxors had come in before the Monarch, which was lucky for the sheets. Had they come in later, they might never have left their packaging.

"One weekend." He was positively giggling. "You spent *five* months getting them, April. And for what? One night?"

"They didn't fit just right." Her mouth was a sliver in the sand. But the storm continued to brew. It stirred behind her pale eyes.

"Did you ever think that maybe things don't have to be so perfect?"

Her eyes narrowed, catlike, and the sliver turned up like a crescent moon. "I seem to be reminded of that every day."

The children never saw Jack shout. Like most children they had no clue that their father had a side unknown to them, the side that made babies and painted well into the night. That's why anytime they heard banging coming from the shed they pictured him as clumsy or imagined him building something. The Jack that they knew wiped up spills and played airplane with mashed potatoes. He made space out of bed sheets on slow summer mornings. The father that they knew was incapable of passion, especially not anger, so when Jack slammed his hand on the counter, then moved in close to April with his hands rolled into tight balls, Piggy whimpered from the corner where the children crouched hidden and watching before scampering like fleeing bugs.

He whispered to her on one breath before following after them. "Happy?"

They were easier to calm than he'd imagined. After all, he and April rarely quarreled beyond a passive-aggressive parley. He assured the children with promises of ice cream and a nice family dinner, chalking the tense interlude up to the heat of the day. Pigg was the hardest sell. Tears still threatened, like dammed-up water, when the children settled down for an afternoon movie.

Wilma Womack was the first thing he saw when he left his secret lady behind. He could kiss her just then. Clarity is strange that way.

"Well, hello there, Just Jack. You look like you won the big sweepstakes or something. Where's his big check, Gussie? Behind his back?"

The golden looked at Jack expectantly, the Laurel to Ms. Womack's Hardy.

"No check." He couldn't help but smile. The woman's delight radiated from her smile skyward, and it wasn't put on. Joy like that couldn't help but be contagious. He pulled his hands from behind his back, wiping rosy pinks from the back of his hand. "I just about finished a project long in the making."

Wilma had been wondering what he did back there. She bit back the urge to ask to see and instead smiled

135

crookedly.

He added, not noticing how she shifted from one foot to the other, "Almost... I've got one more thing to do before it's done." For a second his mind drifted to the task and he was somewhere else. Wilma didn't seem to mind waiting. "What are you two up to this fine evening? A nice supper, perhaps? Gus, you look like a man about town. Heading to a fancy restaurant?" He gave the proud looking young man a brisk rub on the head, to which he replied with a wag of his tongue.

"Gus and I are taking in some air and trying to figure out what to do with all of our extra space."

Jack didn't reply. Instead he rubbed the bristles on his chin wondering what he'd missed.

"My husband..." She looked to her companion for words but he answered only with three deep breaths. She shrugged. "Edgar left."

Mr. Pollack's eyes widened and his shoulders rose in an instinctive shrug. But she waved off any attempt at pity or comfort though his arms looked so inviting.

"The other day, Just Jack." She nodded once at her neighborhood friend whose brow furrowed in concern. "Oh, don't feel bad. It's not a sorry thing, really. And we're not being brave, right Gussie?" Her cheeks dimpled cherub-like as her a smile broke through the tension of potential heartbreak. "I may just have a party."

April was in the bedroom, Solomon tucked under her arm like a wrinkled purse. She was applying some kind of cream under her eyes that stunk of wilted flowers. Her voice was flat and pointed at the ends, like an arrowhead.

"You know, we've been circling around this and I see no reason trying to avoid it." She didn't look at him. She watched in the vanity as if some Homeric drama played out within the reflection. Even the cat seemed rapt with the invisible show behind the glass. "I've given some serious thought to that conversation we had."

His skin felt raw, reddening in anticipation of what was

to come. So this was what it felt like when the knife went in, that gallows feeling before the big drop. He awaited the swish of the guillotine, and though he'd thought he'd feel at peace, it never came. The unease twisted inside him like a serpent.

"I know what I need to do," she added as an afterthought. "I'm getting my eyes lasered."

"I'm sorry?"

"My eyes, Jackson. I'm going to smooth them out. With a laser." Her voice hadn't changed but he felt the challenge. She looked back into the mirror which seemed far more interesting to her than her own words. "You've got your shed. Your little walks in the *fresh air*. You never smell; I'll give you that much." She opened her eyes wide.

"Dr. Volt can do it right in the office." She touched the delicate skin above her cheek. "And then they'll be perfect." She turned to him with exaggerated satisfaction. "Happy?"

He threw up his hands in surrender, which was mistaken for two loose thumbs up as April slipped back into gazing at herself and Solomon in the mirror.

The children were relieved when their parents' earlier promise was fulfilled. Dinner passed without incident and for the most part in silence, not an ill word spoken from either of them. Alton expounded on the intricate details of wormholes in space as Mollie illustrated with black bean paste and salsa verde. Jack could feel the blank space between them like a frigid black hole. But the shed was inviting, and there he felt warm again.

In the shed she waited patiently, her eyes focused in welcome regard, less intense than aware. Her arms were strong but softened with hints of light reflecting from the shoulders. But it was in her cheeks that he found his solace. Those warm cheeks held all the comfort he needed, soft, forgiving. They accepted the world around them, flaws and all.

"Not a tea party," Mrs. Womack had said as they stood

out front, "but a big old barbecue for the entire neighborhood with food and—" She looked thoughtful for a moment then snapped to "—Margaritas! Margaritas and music! I do hope the ladies will come on such short notice." Her eyes focused on him now as they centered the dream spinning round her. "Will you come, Jack?"

She looked girlish and hopeful. To Jack, there seemed but one clear answer to the question before him: "I wouldn't miss it, Wilma."

Wilma's voice sounded in his head like a song long after she'd walked away. It rose and fell in his head like a Viennese waltz set on repeat. "We'll celebrate a new life..." she raised an invisible glass in pantomime salute "...to the little things."

And as she lowered her arm the toast morphed into a wave hello as the new neighbors walked by, a young man and a girl that looked more like a frightened mouse. Wilma smiled and mouthed a greeting to the young couple as they passed.

"Ah, love..." Her focus was on him again and her tone changed. It was as tender as before but it was tinged with a sound more familiar to him, regret. At once he was unsure if she was still talking about her party. "It doesn't have to be perfect, you know."

He looked now at the frame in front of him in all her glory and dropped the brush before taking another stroke. His lady was perfect as she was, and for all intents and purposes, finished. It was he who needed something.

He reached into his secret place and retrieved a match from his pocket. He would savor this all the more because he'd waited so long. And April would never know.

He looked at his lady and relished every inch of what he'd done, to the last impeccable line.

Then he set her ablaze.

ECHO'S WORST NIGHTMARE

*O*ften before the depths of sleep comes a veil of tranquility, a tight line that divides consciousness from the abyss. John lay there sometimes, suspended between the two worlds, his body floating above the covers like a ghost. It was magical in this twilight place. Daphne sometimes joked that he slept like the dead, while she was one to wake with the slightest sound. Once Echo was out, there wasn't much to rouse him from slumber.

Always before the blackness came he saw sparks, fireworks cast against the backdrop of his eyelids, popping in succession, a finale to cap off his day and the indicator that the good sleep was sure to rejuvenate him. Once the sparks were gone, true dreams would begin.

Sometimes he was a boy, back at his father's house, running through the hallways and chasing a bright rubber ball. Other times he stood atop a giant peak, snowflakes dancing off the tip of his nose like a thousand crystal fairies. Tonight his body had the familiar feeling of paralysis, which meant the visions were on the way. He was a stone against the mattress. And then he sank into the down. This was the bed of fancy, a mattress that was both cloud and concrete slab, silky and billowy, warm against his flesh yet cool to his hands. And he could smell pecans and oysters, which in this dream seemed to go together without question. It was a salty scent that was rich in his nostrils and clung to the inside of his lips like a first kiss.

Sleep had overtaken him, of this he was sure. But he dreamed he was dreaming, a disconcerting state, something he hated even in this realm of uncertain elation. He preferred things to be clearer than that, visions where his senses went into overdrive and took him to places where colors exploded and sounds erupted in his ears like summer storms. He wanted snakes playing tubas and stripteases from his love set to vaudeville rag. He wanted foreign languages and velvet tapestries and golden lamps eliciting a curious haze. Yet such subtlety was not forthcoming; this room all too gray, much like his own bedroom when the lights were off.

It seemed a waste to dream of himself in his own bed. But this wasn't his bed, was it? Daphne wasn't here. She was somewhere he could not place, far away, yet he knew that she'd once mattered, like an old thought lost in time.

And then she appeared at the foot of the bed, as if she'd been summoned from thin air, her unmistakable curls set in flaming red bows. Her lips shone like rubies. Echo's drawstring pants had vanished and he lay naked atop his bed, just as Daphne had for years. But he had no one beside him watching for predators and boogeymen. The one eyeing him was not as much watching as she was surveying as he lay paralyzed. The tiny negligee barely covered what was beneath and clung to her hips. This was not Daphne but Annabelle in her prime. She moved like a cat, skin glowing with heat. But she brought the cold with her, too. Her mouth was luscious and frightening all at once. Perhaps it was because he couldn't understand, or perhaps it was because he finally could. He could see her mouth moving, but the sound she emitted was foreign, like no language he'd ever heard.

He didn't know what was more disconcerting, the unnatural way her head inclined and lowered toward his body, or the fact that he was about to have a wet dream. The disgust stirred his insides and his guilt wriggled and squirmed within as if it were a palpable entity. This was not lost on Annabelle. Her face paused over his bellybutton and hovered there. The heat from her cheeks seared his skin.

But that was nothing compared to her hands. She traced the line inside his arm to his chest and down the line of his belly, and he could feel the heat cutting through his skin like a laser, glacial yet torrid as his skin burst open in agony. But she left not a scratch. In this world pain meant nothing because it left no mark.

Her hands kneaded him above his pelvic bone and down to his inner thigh, and he felt as if his head would rupture like an overripe fruit. He could feel his breathing quicken as his eyes focused on hers. Her murmuring matched the primal heartbeats that sounded from within him, a pain they shared.

Her nails looked like fire as she kissed playfully at him through the space between her fingers. A flick of her tongue, and then those hands were all over his belly. They traced hot lines over his skin and he smelled the scent of searing flesh. But no mark was left. He felt only the aching he'd tried to hide, the pain that hurt too much to recognize.

His voice broke through the cloud like a bell: "I want it." Annabelle smiled in recognition. Her mouth descended but did not touch him. It hovered like a heat lamp burning below his navel and his eyes focused on the surroundings that both confused and welcomed. He could see the night sky, and the stars blinked at him like watching eyes, and he felt relief descend upon him like a weight had lifted. He was hers now. That much was clear.

She licked at her red hands and laid her face across his exposed body, nuzzling at him more lovingly than before and taking pieces of him for herself. She stroked him and mumbled nothings that somehow made sense now. He gazed dumbly as she pulled him through her hair, rubbing him upon her cheeks and lips.

And as if summoned by lust and longing, Daphne sat in a jacket of bone, creamy and smooth, matching those of the other ladies who sat around him. Mrs. Granger sat at the head like the queen. Annabelle sat at his shoulders, abandoning his crotch for a fresh crumpet that she offered to the other ladies. She'd traded in her lacy nightie for silk and linen.

At his feet sat Daphne, placed so naturally, and so at home with these women. She nodded easily as they discussed the weather. They talked around him and about him as if he weren't there at all.

"He's divine."

"Irresistible."

"Can't keep him all to yourself..."

Only loathing remained as Daphne stared at the place where Annabelle had been. Without hesitation she lifted the knife and plunged it between his legs. She cut into him like a cake and handed slices to each lady. Thick red jelly dripped from the knife that she wiped clean on Annabelle's crumpet.

They joked and laughed and ate him alive as he sat in openmouthed silence, a bizarre twist on a video he'd seen as a child. Tom Petty's macabre Mad Hatter ate a helpless Alice cake while Echo was still young enough to dream of happy endings. He couldn't see Daphne this way, smiling behind layers of lipstick and talking of topiaries. Her hair was pulled taut like Mrs. Granger's. Her lips lacquered like Annabelle's, she spoke of her garden with a combination of fervor and urgency, which made Abigail applaud. She sprinkled her anecdotes with trite stereotypes. She looked at the wreckage of what was once his lower body.

"Is this what you wanted?"

A scream exploded in his ears. He was sure that when he opened his eyes the gruesome remains of his own skull would be soiling the pristine surroundings of his fancy. But the screams of panic that stopped the macabre tea party were not in fact his, they were unmistakably Daphne's.

It was remarkable how quickly the cobwebs of a nightmare could clear when reality was far more disturbing than the darkest dream. He ran so quickly down the steps that he didn't hear the crackling underfoot.

She was hunched low to the ground with her back to him. Her head was so close to the floor that she looked savage, and if she did notice that he'd come into the room, she didn't show it. He spoke as he always did when her hair went wild and her eyes abandoned the world.

"Daphne, what are you doing?"

Her head moved to an angle that made his stomach lurch.

He clicked on a small table lamp hoping the light would bring her back.

When she turned to him he saw the blood all over her palms. Tiny bits of paper and string littered his feet. What he'd taken as strange shadows were cutouts taped to the wall in odd positions, some hanging by a thread. The symmetry was unnerving.

"Butterflies..." She shot out the word out as if it had been fired from a gun. "Those poor, poor butterflies that never get to fly."

She was on her feet now, circling, still cutting perfect circles in paper with the kitchen shears. She didn't flinch when the scissors nicked her fingers.

"All those butterflies: all dead."

Her hair was streaked in places and when she grabbed at the top of her head a new sticky red spot appeared. Tears and blood left her face looking like a Dickens' orphan, and her lip was swollen where she'd either been bitten or stuck with the sharp kitchen shears.

"They never get out into the world. No chance." Her eyes filled with tears and her breath came too quickly for her words. She dropped the shears without flinching, even when the point dug into the top of her foot. She held herself like a straightjacket and looked at Echo with eyes that made his soul go cold, then she wept so hard that the last word she uttered was barely understandable. But he knew what it was: "Baby."

Dreams aside, he knew what he had to do. The real nightmare was just beginning.

FAIRY GODMOTHERS

*"D*o you think she's set out sandwiches?"

Annabelle clucked her teeth at the woman on her left. "Abigail, she's in a state. I don't think she's set out anything."

"I think the both of you should let me do the talking, all right?" April had the uncanny talent to give an order in the form of a question. Her smile matched the crescent necklace that lay perfectly on her collarbone, flawless like the rest of her. The women moved together in a cloud of color.

"You're quiet. What's the matter with you?" April bristled but her companion was distant and answered in a far off, undetermined way.

Agnes dragged behind; her countenance matched her pace. "Me? Nothing... Eliot is having a bad day." She paused, biting her bottom lip like a little girl worried about a monster beneath her bed.

"You didn't seem so worried about him before, honey. Don't start now. It's unbecoming." Annabelle was brazen, speaking like a Mae West dame with no time for nonsense, which only served to agitate the thoughtful mouse in the green garden hat that flitted nervously beside her.

"Annabelle, really..." April slipped a friendly arm around her shoulder. Abigail's eyebrows lifted as she spoke over her friend. "Never mind Annabelle. She's *hungry;* that's all. Isn't that right Annabelle?" She prodded with her words. "You didn't mean anything by it, right?"

The one with the hips for sin smacked her slick lips together already losing interest in the conversation at hand.

"I don't know what she's thinking," she said looking over at the heavy set woman in the bucket hat across the street that fawned over the golden dog with the bouncy ears. "A party?" She sniffed. "What gives her the right? April, did she clear it with us?"

She'd been handing out invitations since yesterday's afternoon tea, and like Abigail's crab dip, it didn't sit well. The woman in gold stopped dead, reaching into one of the several zippers that decked her romper. Her large sunglasses looked like molten metal, and her hat gleamed in the sun. She looked like she was striking a hero's pose until the clattering feet of the others stopped in time just behind her. She unfolded the crumpled paper as if it were coated in primordial slime. "Of course she didn't clear it with us. Who would clear this?"

The women huddled around her like a pack of hyenas.

"Is that a pig?" Even Agnes took an interest, a tiny smirk breaking the tragic mask she'd worn all morning.

"A grinning pig," April corrected. "And nothing about this is funny. She's clearly defaced one our flyers." It was a fuzzy copy at best, but Mrs. Womack had taken the time to construct the smiling brute from construction paper as well as a sombrero and numerous flags before pasting them on the Twin Oaks flyer. The finished product was a breathtaking spectacle to say the least.

"What is a Fiesta de la Libertad? Is that some kind of holiday?" Abigail cupped a hand over her eye and tilted her head to the side in such a way that she now resembled the golden retriever headed their way.

Mrs. Womack was too busy to notice, smiling widely and talking to the dark skinned woman, the one with the husband that played guitar. She handed her a long thin envelope that looked as though it had been dipped in glitter, no doubt stuffed with one of these atrocities. That dog of hers took three steps toward the ladies then, as if thinking the better, headed back to the floppy woman with the sparkly envelope.

"Honestly, ladies, how long are we going to let this go on?"

Annabelle broke in as if the answer was as clear as the swine in front of them and moved past the scene without an afterthought. "We'll take care of it."

She grabbed April's elbow and whispered something in her ear. April nodded in approval and peeled away from her companions. She tipped her hat like a giant coin at the two women but ignored the dog as she approached.

"She'll talk some sense into her," Annabelle assured, and Abigail quietly mumbled several suggestions as Agnes dropped behind, reassuming her maudlin stare.

"Would you look at that tall drink of water?"

From behind Adam could pass for another person.

"That's my son, Annabelle."

She winked. "That boy has really come into his own." She inclined her head so her cherry sunhat dipped like a satellite dish. "Good morning, Adam. You're looking well."

"Good morning," he said respectfully.

"How's Dad?"

"He's resting now. Bit of a battle this morning getting him to drink. I'm starting to wonder if it's worth all the fight." He tried not to move his lips and lowered his voice. "I don't want to see him suffer." He wasn't begging but emphatic. "He deserves better than that."

"I know." His mother's voice was suddenly small, no hint of the trademark siren song. "We'll talk later, Adam. I have to go now."

He rubbed his hands together looking confused and frustrated. "It's not like I'm going anywhere," he said.

The Elm Cottage was a white dot that marked the eastern gate of Twin Oaks. It was as picturesque in person as it had been when it sat atop Calliope's cake. The Harbages kept it neat and fresh with tiny flowers outside the windows. For all intents, it was perfect, not a blade of grass out of place, or an indent on the welcome mat. The newlyweds' home was a clean slate, and the ladies waited on the front steps.

Abigail didn't knock. She called inside through the screen when she saw the door was slightly open.

"Daphne, are you in there? Hello?" She bent her head birdlike to determine if there was movement or response. "I brought you some things."

The man's voice answered from upstairs, followed by the conspicuous sound of frantic last minute tidying.

Annabelle pulled the waist of her dress tight, then a quick lift so that she was overflowing from the bodice. Abigail reached into the large side pocket of her bright overalls and extracted a thick plastic baggie tied with a silver string. Agnes stood on the landing.

"What's the holdup, Aggie?" Annabelle motioned for her to come up the stairs. "Something stuck to your shoe?"

Agnes hung her head low like an invisible weight dangled around her neck. "I don't think I can do this."

Annabelle could hear Echo clamoring on the other side of the door. Soft thuds of flung pillows punctuated long sweeps of broom bristles against hardwood.

"Just a second, ladies," he called.

"Do what?" Now Annabelle had turned her back to the front door to peer down at Agnes who was barely mouthing words over a clenched whisper. "*I'm not going in there.*"

Annabelle descended the steps in one motion and held Agnes' face in one hand so she had no choice but to look at her. "Like hell you're not."

Abigail squeaked twice like a shorted car alarm.

"Sorry to keep you waiting, ladies; won't you come in?" He cleared his throat, holding the door for Annabelle. She wasted no time, and as little space, as she shimmied past him. Abigail gave a friendly wave. He looked like he hadn't slept in days but even so kept chivalry alive while waiting for Agnes to bring up the rear.

The ladies could see immediately what had kept him up. He'd tried his best to scrub the bloody handprints from the wall. They overlapped at the thumbs making the distinctive shape recognizable. It matched the paper cutouts that hung from the ceiling.

"I like your butterflies." Had this come from anyone else Echo would suspect sarcasm, but Abigail's smile was childlike and her admiration sincere. She was beside Daphne on the loveseat with a hand on her knee. "They're really beautiful," she said squeezing Daphne's shoulder. She dared not grab her by the hand. "Do you like these?" She pointed to the cheerful flowers blanketing her overalls. "They're kiwi Cymbidiums; very hard to spell, but pretty. Like your butterflies. Delicate, too..." She traced the lines of the flowers and urged Daphne to do the same, but she didn't move.

Daphne shot Echo a look and whispered to her friend behind a raised hand.

"Please, take a seat. Can I get you something?"

When Agnes declined he turned to Annabelle: "Can we speak privately for a second?"

Annabelle's eyes flickered and Echo was surprised when she obliged with courtesy and grace. "Yes, of course." She stood an arm's length away from him and though her eyes told a different story, she kept her hands to herself.

When they were out of earshot, tucked away into the booth that sat in the kitchen, Echo's shoulders slumped and he let out an exhausted sigh. His relief was transparent, and still Annabelle kept her distance.

"I want to thank you for coming. You ladies are like a dream come true right now." His eyes sagged as if pain pulled them at the edges. "I didn't know where else to turn." The tiredness saturated his words like heavy oil. "I don't want to leave her alone."

She leaned over the table and flashed more than her pearly whites. "We take care of our own." She could smell the coconut soap on his skin tinged with the fresh sweat he'd worked up in his attempt to speed clean. She touched his hand and caught herself before he could recoil. But his hand remained in hers, the grip firm.

His weakness was apparent. The circles under his eyes made him look years older than he was. The scruff along his jawline shadowed his face and darkened him even in the cheery brightness of this perfect kitchen. He was weak, easy for the taking, and his need was palpable. Her mind swirled in the scent of him, but her orders had been clear.

Abigail made light conversation and pretended to ignore the gouges and cuts along Daphne's hands. They weren't intentional. She could see that in the zigzags and polka dots that marred her fingers and palms. But they *were* the accidental punctures of passion. She was lost somewhere in those Monarchs and Swallowtails.

Annabelle returned with a steaming kettle on a tray with Echo close behind. They nodded to Abigail in unison. She inhaled sharply as if surprised, one small squeak escaping before she jumped to action

"We're going to let this steep for a minute." She lifted a silver pocket watch that looked older than all of them combined from her rear overall pocket. "Now..."

No one spoke. Abigail's loud breathing marked rhythm. Agnes stared at her feet. Annabelle looked at Echo from the corner of her eye with restrained longing, but he didn't notice. His eyes were on the bloody girl on the couch, the one who shivered every so often though the room was warm and bright.

Abigail moved liked a bee, back and forth between packets and cups, pouring herbs over the steeping brew. "You drink this with a little sea salt." She moved swiftly to Daphne's side. "It's for your nerves," she assured, adding one elaborate pour from a crystal decanter. "Some honey helps, too."

Daphne's eyes were wide and empty. Whether or not she acknowledged any of them was a mystery. When she was like this it was hard to tell. But Abigail had reached for her hands and held them, though her wounds would no doubt color her white flowers crimson. She cupped them in her own around the steaming brew and said in a voice so unlike her usual optimistic singsong. "Drink..."

Daphne drank. And Echo's eyes caught Annabelle's not in an awkward glance of stolen desire but in gratitude. Her wink told him that she knew she was right, and that he'd made the right call.

"Are you ladies going to be all right?" he asked in the lowest whisper. Daphne had fallen asleep quickly, just as Abigail had promised.

"We'll take very good care of her." The two responded in unison though they didn't look at one another. Abigail sat beside Daphne, stroking her hair like a mother, though the two looked like strange mirror images. Annabelle looked out the front window at the neighborhood.

Agnes sat quietly, rubbing at the back of her neck. She moved once to wave goodbye to Echo as he left them behind.

"I won't be gone more than an hour." He looked like some of the pain had been relieved. His eyes looked like they were seeing more clearly. "Thank you. I don't know how to repay you."

She winked, and then assured in earnest, "She's in good hands." But something had obstructed her view.

"Oh my God; she's at it again."

"I thought April had talked to her." Abigail's voice was bright and sunny as she traced the lines of Daphne's hair with her fingertips.

"She did. Evidently it didn't work. She's sticking those things in mailboxes." Her voice was low, like a threatened animal, and shook with the sound of impending strike. "Agnes, perhaps you should bring Mrs. Womack something? A basket of muffins..." Annabelle's eyes shone. "One of your special baguettes, perhaps?"

For the first time all morning Agnes looked up at the other ladies. "No."

"No baguette? Or no muffin, dear? Which do you think will be more effective?"

Agnes rose to her feet and spoke low to protect Daphne. "I'm not bringing that woman anything."

Annabelle laughed mirthlessly, her eyes never leaving the woman in blue. "You're not making any sense."

"I'm done with this." Agnes's eyes were cold and steely, any hint of tears long dried in certainty. "No more."

But still Annabelle questioned: "Do you know what you're saying?"

Agnes whispered, "I never wanted to hurt anyone."

THREE WITCHES

*"G*ood morning star shine!"

Daphne sat up in bed looking more like the girl she once was than the woman she'd been for the past few days.

"How're you feeling sleepyhead?"

Her hands were slathered in a rough, thick coating that felt like sand and water. Plush cotton gloves stretched over her hands spreading relief from her fingers to her wrists. She nodded at Abigail, clearly the Florence Nightingale who'd come during her slumber, clearing the fog from her brain and the sleep from her eyes. "I feel good." She stretched.

Annabelle and Agnes were in the kitchen. She could hear the first woman talking as if fire shot from her eyes, all emotion and heat. But she was so relieved to feel the cool air against her skin as Abigail peeled off the gloves that she hadn't given it a second thought. Her hands were clean and smooth against the fabric. Not a blemish or scar remained. The wounds had melted with her nightmares as she slept away the hours.

"It's a miracle."

"A touch of beeswax and tea tree oil and red clay from the mountains." She was proud of herself, happy that her new friend looked better.

"It's amazing. Abigail. Thank you."

The lithe one in green hopped off the couch like a wind-up toy and landed on one foot in a graceful turn. "And that's not all. I hope you don't mind, but we brought you a little something. I think it should fit." She eyeballed Daphne, hands at her own waist, measuring herself to her friend in approximation, grabbing a garment bag from where it hung on the banister. "I hope you like it." She pulled the skirt and jacket out cautiously, waiting for Daphne's response. "I thought this color would suit you." Her shoulders dropped in relief when she saw Daphne smiling. "It's called blushing rose."

Daphne ran a hand over the smooth silk shell that hid inside the crisp jacket.

"Try it on. Let's see how it looks."

She crinkled her nose girlishly. It felt good to smile. "Should we tell them we'll be gone for a while?"

"They'll figure it out." Abigail shrugged. And without a second thought the two scampered upstairs like schoolgirls.

"We were right about this color. You look great. We thought maybe plum, but there used to be a lady who wore things like that. It didn't really work out for her."

"What do you mean? What happened?"

"Nothing serious; she just moved. She's not with us anymore." Her eyes darted, unsure. "The lady from the big house over there," she stammered, changing the subject. They weren't supposed to discuss Mrs. MacMillan. "So, you look great!"

Her reflection looked like a different girl peering out from the long mirror.

"This is really for me?"

"If you want it..." Annabelle appeared in the doorway.

"All you have to do is ask." She came to Daphne with arms open. "You're one of us now."

"Not officially," Agnes chimed from outside the door. They had found their way to her after all. "Not a lady, until the first formal meeting." Her words were urgent and hushed. "And you're nobody until you've had your private meeting with the president." There was strain in her voice. "Those are the rules." Daphne was too pleased with her new suit and pretty pink pillbox hat to notice the looks shot straight through the woman speaking.

Agnes led the way, wringing her hands with each step down the stairs. April was removing her large brimmed hat, placing it gingerly on the sofa like a baby.

"Well, well. Look at you, Mrs. Harbage. Looking fabulous after all!" She clapped her hands together holding them just beneath her heart. "Lovely! Simply wonderful! Feeling better?"

"Yes, you've all been so nice to me."

Agnes, though silent, had been efficient in her removal of the butterflies; and if Daphne had noticed, she didn't show it. The room was back to its showroom perfection. And the leggy woman dressed in gold gave it the appearance of a magazine ad, just the way April liked it.

"So you want to tell us what happened with that woman out there?" Annabelle motioned dismissively at the big picture window. Mrs. Womack's silhouette was unmistakable against the sky.

"I reminded her that all neighborhood parties need to be planned through the proper channels," April spoke through a veneer of sparkling teeth, partially out of habit, partially because her jaw had clenched at the mention of Mrs. Womack.

"And what did she say?" Annabelle prodded.

"She said that it will start at 4:00, and that we should bring some dip or fresh fruit for her trademark party *wafflitos*."

Abigail let out a sound that was fully gasp and zero

squeak: "We're going to have to tell Mrs. Granger."

"I think not. Shoot the messenger. Been there, and it wasn't fun." Annabelle's hips swayed as she paced the room. "Or we could handle it ourselves."

It was Agnes who gasped now: "No. Not again. I won't. I can't. You can't make me do that again."

"Do what?" April asked.

Annabelle cautioned, "This isn't the time, Agnes."

"I just wanted my own success. I didn't want Adam to be in his father's shadow anymore. I wanted to be able to say, this is mine." She muttered. "I didn't want anything to happen to anyone."

"Well, I didn't say I wanted to be a raging nymphomaniac, did I? Did I?" Annabelle questioned, hand on hip. And even in outrage she looked like she'd walked out of an old dirty magazine. "All I wanted was to be sexy and vital." She sniffed. "And now I'm the goddamn whore of Babylon." And then she walked off toward the kitchen muttering as Daphne had the night before. "I'm starving!"

Abigail, holding Daphne's hand, attempted a whisper unsuccessfully. "That lady in purple didn't work out either. We handled it: Agnes, Annabelle, and me. Couple mushrooms and essence of nightshade. Now no one wears purple. Shame about her roses, though. Have to look into that when we can."

"Abigail!" Agnes and Annabelle chided in unison. April listened with an open mouth not quite processing what she'd heard. "You think Abigail *wanted* to be a simpleton?" Her gaze was fixed on Agnes, accusing, forgetting anyone else was in the room. "She wanted *youth*, dear Aggie. And that comes at a price."

"You get used to it." Abigail shrugged as if she were talking about possible rain.

April, used to running things, stood in the center of the room, a deep crease running the center of her forehead, splitting it in two. This is where she stood months ago, controlling the crowd, rallying hungry buyers to clamor for a chance at a home in Twin Oaks. Now she barely had control of her own faculties. There was a tremor in her voice that reminded her of another lifetime.

"What are you two talking about?"

"Oh, that's right. You don't know that half of it. You haven't been around that long, have you Ms. VP?"

April looked from one lady to the next unsure of what she was seeing.

"We all want something, April, don't we?"

The three women encircled her. Daphne was too taken with herself again to notice the panic. She looped a stray hair over her ear without a worry in the world, admiring her reflection in the old grandfather clock.

Agnes's head dropped like a doll's. Her voice was one note of defeat.

"What was it that you wanted, April?"

When they adjourned that first meeting she'd never said it out loud, but it had stirred inside her. It had from the first time she stepped through the gates of Twin Oaks. It echoed in her ear with her own heartbeat: *Control.*

She could see Mrs. Granger's savant face looking at her as they closed the circle. She could feel the woman's icy grip, like a vice around her wrist. And she didn't seem to mind it. She felt her back straighten, her shoulders lift; her voice spoke to the women around her.

"We'll take care of her..." The ladies stepped out from in front of her so that her view was clear.

"Daphne, dear, what is it you want?"

She turned away from the clock and saw the circle for the first time.

When Echo came home he saw a ring of women in his sitting room, and at its center was Daphne, made over like a doll. She laughed lightly, like she had when they were back on the islands, as free as she was before the nightmare had begun. She was smiling and chatting, a vision from her pink hat to her matching shoes, just one of the ladies.

BARK AT THE MOON

Mrs. Womack stood on a chair between the pig and the bar, a feat that made the balancing act of her sombrero look tame, and held up what looked like an ancient megaphone from a bygone era.

"Hello! Can everyone hear me okay?" she tested. "I just want to thank everyone who came to my first official Fiesta de la Libertad. On behalf of Gussie and myself, I say from the bottom of my heart, drink up, eat well, and have a great time! And hooray for liberty!" She took one step before remembering one last note, and lingered there, one foot hanging like bait while she finished. "Also, thanks to Ben Chalmers for this megaphone and the tables and chairs, extra linens and miscellaneous décor."

Ben and Bea sat at a long wooden table laid with Mexican and American flags and checked tablecloths. It was a plethora of festive colors that didn't quite belong but somehow worked. Much like the people who attended the party, Wilma found a way to bring them together. Bea couldn't remember the last time that Ben had come out, but here he sat, sipping margaritas and munching on *wafflitos* stuffed with chocolate cream and lime marmalade. He'd saved several seats for whoever might show up, but the smile on his face hinted that he was hoping for a select few.

"Hey!" The voice came from the sidewalk as if he'd willed them here. Dawn climbed the grassy incline between the street and Wilma's festive world. She had a look on her face that could easily have been confusion or discomfort. It was hard to guess.

"Honey, you look fine." Bea knew it was the latter.

"I thought it was a theme party." Her shoulders lifted as she inadvertently reached for the plump rose behind her ear. "I feel silly."

"You're a knockout, kid. I don't know what you're talking about." Ben stood and brought her hands up in front of her so he could take in the sight. "Look around you. You think anyone feels foolish here?"

Chili pepper lights were strung from the pergola. Bright streamers were tucked between the slats like a multicolored spider web. Chubby glitter pigs hung from the barbecue grill and off tables like disco balls. Mrs. Womack altered a cardboard cutout of a baseball player so he looked like a mariachi in red, white, and blue. The woman herself wore a sombrero and teetered on a chair in an attempt to hang a plump piñata.

"All they had was unicorns. You think we can make it look mean? I kind of feel bad beating this up," she said to Smedley Johnson, who normally collected recyclables on the highway outside the gates. The old timer smiled and downed his drink, stowing the can in a pile he kept under the table.

"Hello, Mrs. Ringhaus," she called from across the yard with an exuberant wave.

Dawn felt less self-conscious already, seeing the guests milling around with cut-out fans and paper parasols sticking out of their drinks. But she hadn't worn a dress like this in years.

"Mommy took a special trip to get a dress," Lucy said.

"Is that right?" Bea asked.

"I think you look really pretty, Mom," Becca said.

"We got these." Lucy twirled and her ruffled skirt made the sound of flowers blowing in the wind.

"I thought we'd be festive," Dawn said slinking into the seat next to Ben.

"You're a hot tamale, kid. A real firecracker!" He playfully pushed Dawn's arm and her face bloomed in pinks and reds that favored her pretty sundress. "You all look great."

Her eyes darted from the far end of the yard to the pig, then to the bar.

"Looking for someone?" Ben prodded.

"Of course not." She adjusted her flower again. "Just seeing who showed. She has a nice turnout."

"Right." Ben winked. "Let me get you a drink. Girls?"

But Lucy and Becca had spotted their new friends from down the street and were bouncing in their seats.

"Can we?" Becca pleaded.

"Go ahead," Dawn said with a smile, and the girls darted away.

Bea coughed like she was choking and Dawn jumped at the sound.

"Is this seat taken?" The warm voice brought Dawn's cheeks back to the three shades of pink they'd been seconds before. She turned to see Adam. His flowered shirt was loud and loose, nothing like the muted t-shirts she'd seen him wear. His hair was pushed in the same direction as if it had seen a comb. And what's more, he carried a flower that looked eerily similar to the one in her hair.

"I thought you might like this." He placed the rose in front of Dawn. His other hand rubbed the top of his head unintentionally, his face matching hers in color.

"For me?" She placed a hand on top of the flower.

"Thank you."

"I thought I'd be festive." His smile was crooked, and he was clumsy pulling too hard on the plastic chair as he sat.

"Look who's here," Ben called, his hands full of *cerveza* and frosted party glasses.

Behind him in the yard the girls were discussing UFO's with the Pollack children.

The two newlyweds from down the street walked arm in arm and headed straight for Mrs. Womack.

"John and Daphne!" she exclaimed. "I'm so happy you could make it. Can I get you a tequila?" She threw back her head and took a long swallow, her face contorted like an old apple. "Whoo doggie! None of this for Gussie!" She came to the young couple with arms extended, sombrero cocked firmly to the right.

"No, thank you, Mrs. Womack." Echo smiled, taking her hand and shaking it.

She continued as he spoke: "We're just passing through."

Daphne's eyes took in everything like a newborn baby. The worry lines and furrows had disappeared and she looked around at the glittery pigs and mariachis with wonder.

"Oh, stay a while, would you? Please! You'll miss all the fun!"

Echo loved the thought of a party, the possibility of seeing Daphne dance and twirl like she used to. But despite her smiles and newfound glow, he feared pushing her too hard, too soon. She did look beautiful tonight, her face made up and her hair done. He hadn't seen her run a brush through her hair in longer than he'd care to admit. And her smile was mesmerizing. What he wouldn't do to keep things this way.

"Maybe a burger?" he suggested and Wilma clapped her hands like a schoolgirl. Daphne moved forward toward the woman where for a moment, confused, Echo thought she might be attempting some sort of embrace. Instead she shot out the words like darts: "I have a message for you Wilma Womack." The voice was cold and didn't match the rosy cheeks of the speaker.

"What's that?"

Daphne was robotic and terse. "The ladies of the association will not be attending this function. This spectacle you have staged in your yard is a mockery of Twin Oaks." She didn't nod or blink or acknowledge the woman who stood in front of her. "You have been warned."

"Warned?" Wilma was perplexed.

"Heed our warning," Daphne advised, turning on one foot and walking away.

Echo stood as flummoxed as the woman in the sideways sombrero. He put an apologetic hand on her shoulder. "I'm sorry, Mrs. Womack." He sighed. "It's probably too soon." He didn't want to explain. "We're," he searched for the right words, "going through something right now. Please forgive Daphne. She really doesn't know what she's saying."

He walked away from Wilma and continued until he and Daphne were down the dirt hill and back on the sidewalk, safely tucked away from the *Fiesta de la Libertad.* But Daphne's voice was loud in a clear-cut monotone: "I know exactly what I'm saying."

Wilma passed by Hettie, the nurse she ran into down the street, and the Flanders twins from her podiatrist's office, offering them some queso dip and some sour apple popsicles, but when all had declined she found herself back at Mr. Tequila, who was always down for a good time.

"I say we crank up our music!" she urged and sent the cashier from the Quik Stop inside to adjust the volume on her speakers.

"Hello, Wilma." His voice was muddled over the music but she'd know it anywhere.

"Just Jack!"

His face brightened hers.

"I told you I wouldn't miss it." He took in the sights, admiring it all. "This is something else, Wilma. Now this is a good time."

She wasn't buying it. For all of her work and effort half the neighborhood hadn't shown. He must have sensed her disappointment because he shifted from one foot to the other and grabbed at his arm, uncomfortably.

"I'm sorry April couldn't make it. She's got a lot going on with the...." He reached. She'd screamed at him like a crazed banshee when he'd said where he was going, with their children no less. He could see the veins bulging in her neck, and the narrowed eyes of that stupid cat.

"Association," Wilma finished for him. "They don't approve. They won't be here." She sniffed. But he was. And the children were playing. Gus was having a good time. If she was going to take her chance, this was the time. "Would you like some tequila, Just Jack?"

He looked around the yard, at the grinning decorations and fancy hats. He saw Alton laughing with a young girl who seemed very interested in what he had to say. Mollie drew on a clay pot with a stick for Pigg who clapped wildly at the cartoonish piggy floating in space. There was nothing perfect about it, but damn if it didn't make the kid happy.

"What the hell? Line 'em up, Wilma."

By sundown the children's voices echoed through the streets; games of pirates and princesses morphed into archeological adventures and the exploration of space. Ned Frehling, the butcher responsible for the pig, necked with Miss Vance from the library. Each had eyed the other from afar for so long that it only took a little *Libertad* to bring them together.

"Why don't you play us something?" Dawn asked Mr. Chalmers. "You brought that thing for a reason, didn't you?"

"Go ahead, Ben; play us something nice."

He pulled his beat-up Harmony from underneath the table and shrugged. "I might as well."

He strummed a somber tune that floated on the air like bubbles. It stopped Ms. Womack in mid-piñata-strike. She froze there like a statue.

Miss Vance pulled away from her paramour, swaying with the music, woozy in the moonlight. She looked deep into his eyes and mouthed something that only he could hear. Even the children took pause in their game, the girls twirling like music box dancers, Pigg hopping from one foot to the other.

Jack was smiling at his children when the buzzing started. He ignored it when it vibrated in his ears.

"Another!" Shouted Lucy. "Another, another!"

Ben motioned to Adam, who picked up a set of maracas and tossed one to each girl.

"May I?" He ran to Mrs. Womack and pulled an empty ice tub from her veggie bar, then flipped it upside down. "And a one, and a two, and a..."

Ben played a fast rock and roll, and the kids went wild. Adam drummed along with a fiery beat that got the whole party up and out of their chairs and dancing on the back lawn. And amid all this a strange sound came from the far back corner where they stood.

Gustav howled a melody above the music like a ghostly soprano. It was mournful yet celebratory, reaching into the crowd so they heard. It made Wilma think of the future. It made Jack regret the past. It made Dawn turn and look at Adam as if she didn't give a damn about the world around her. Ben couldn't put a finger on what note it was, but it was so beautiful that he couldn't match it.

And then the buzzing became more insistent. Jack could feel it in his ears. It shook him above and below.

"Hello?" He held a hand over his free ear, hating that he was missing the party to be fielding this call. "No. No, I'm not. You come here and do it if it's that important to you." He paced back to the party. "Oh, I see. No, that's fine. I will. But then I'm done."

No one could hear what he said to Mrs. Womack, but it didn't make the task any easier for him. Her shoulders slumped and her lip jutted out like a heartbreak that he couldn't fix. And all the while he felt like a class A heel.

Her lips barely moved. "A formal complaint?" He nodded. "Against me?" She turned to take a step but didn't know where to go. "I don't make a peep in this neighborhood. I don't bother a soul." She took off her hat and smoothed her hair. Her dimples dipped and stretched as her face went from frown to wince to serious yet again. "And they want to discuss whether or not I belong here?"

She scanned the dancing bodies and smiling faces that graced her yard and her face stretched into a wide, amused grin.

"Do you all think it's too loud out here?" she hollered to the uproarious answer to the contrary. "Me neither," she sang it into the clouds, grabbing the piñata that wouldn't break off of its string and bashing it against the bar. "I say, who cares if it's too loud?" she added in a staccato shout that marked each pounding of the sad unicorn against the white concrete at her sandals. "I." She pounded. "Say." She hit it again about the smiling face and neck. "Who." She had it now. "Cares!" A kaleidoscope of color flew out of the wounded toy, sugar drops flying to the ground like tiny grenades. She picked up a handful of sour candies and threw them into the yard. "Suck on this, association!"

But that wasn't all. Gustav looked on as his master danced through the crowd of revelers, riling them to shout hip-hip hoorays in honor of the day.

"Thank you. Thank you all for coming," she announced. "To celebrate this day!" She descended the dirt hill onto the sidewalk below. "To celebrate with me!" She stood in the middle of the street now, screaming, sombrero askew. "Loud and proud, we celebrate! Do you hear me? Do you hear me, ladies? Is it too loud for you?"

Mr. Chalmers kicked up his playing, intensifying the challenge that had been laid out. The tune was fast and as furious as Wilma had become, drawing the eyes of partygoers and curious children alike.

She spread her hands out to the sky. "It's such a beautiful night. Look at that moon. Do you like it?" She screamed so that her face looked like a beet against the backdrop of black sky.

And then, in answer, Gus howled. He howled not in the unearthly angel voice he'd howled before, but in an a primitive, feral way that made Wilma stand up straight and tall like a soldier receiving an order.

"If you don't like the noise, then you can enjoy the view!" she screamed, and in an instant dropped her flowered shorts around her ankles, bottom white and bare to the homeowners who opted out of the barbecue. "Are you happy now?" She chuckled as she looked out between her own legs. She was surprisingly limber.

Wilma was exhausted when it was through, as was her companion. He panted at her side, leaning into her bare leg as she lifted her shorts back up around her waist. Not one of the women had opened a door. Not a curtain wavered. Nor did a phone vibrate in a pocket. There was no hint that she'd made even a dent in the wall that separated the ladies from herself, when all she'd wanted was for them to notice.

"Hey, what do you say to some fireworks?" Ben stood on top of the hill and called down to her as if the previous spectacle hadn't occurred. "Who wants some?" he urged. "I got some good ones."

Wilma pulled back her hair from where it stuck to the side of her face. Her guests ate and laughed, but not at her. They banged away at piñatas and danced. Not one stopped to make a fuss or complain.

"Yes, we can set up here. And the little ones can go here. And we also need. What do I need?" She steadied her chin with her hand. "Sangria!" The moon had started to sway. "Oh, and fireworks!"

"I've got a whole box of them back home, Wilma. I'll just pop in to get them." He took a few steps toward his guitar to pack it up then stopped, hand clutching his back. "Hey, Dawn, why don't you and Adam go and pick them up? It's a nice night for an evening stroll." He took the young man aside with instructions, placing the key in his hands like a sacred vestige.

"Yes, I think that's a fine idea. We can set up over here." The gears had started to turn and Wilma was in the center of the yard triangulating distances and viewing angles.

Jack, who was feeling the sway of the sky as much as Wilma, searched for a minute alone with his woozy friend. He bobbed between the mailman and a lady named Flo who sold fresh vegetables on Sundays. He ducked under a drooping pig snout that almost kissed him smack on the mouth. And then he saw her, half-slumped over a pile of freshly cut radishes and a bowl of dill cream.

She'd laid her head beside the vegetables and closed her eyes as if to sleep. She let out a peaceful sigh.

"Taking a break?" He smiled.

"Oh, Just Jack, hello," she said. The startle had sent a shockwave to her head and her hand followed. "I think my *Libertad* may have caught up with me." Her cheeks were cherub-like even when they were hellfire red, and she hung her head self-consciously. "I'm a little embarrassed."

"Don't be," he said.

Her eyes drifted to the street in front of her house, then to the ground. "I didn't want you to think I was a fool."

"I don't think you're a fool, Wilma. I don't think you're a fool at all." Jack looked at the smooth lines of her face, the round curves of her arms and her eyes glistening with sorrows, and the hope of a brighter day. They were in and out of focus, with pupils like plump olives. The swinging cadence and volume had left his voice. He was tempered by what he saw. "You're probably not going to remember this tomorrow but," he placed a finger under her chin and lifted her eyes to his, "I think you're perfect."

FIREWORKS

The walk to back to the Chalmers' house wasn't long but Adam found himself taking short steps in order to extend their time together. She was beautiful this evening, with her spaghetti straps and the flower in her hair, and so carefree with her smile. The sangria had colored her cheeks pink and she spoke with a lilt in her voice only found when one has been freed of the young ones she has in tow. There was an air of ease to her words that he hadn't heard before. He had a lump in his throat the size of a fist.

"Some party, huh?"

"Yeah, pretty interesting." She inclined her head his way when she spoke and their arms brushed. "Luckily, the girls were so taken with Ben that they didn't notice the other show."

He fumbled for the key, reaching harder into his pocket than he'd intended. "Here we are."

They walked over the clean sandstones of the Chalmers' entry path like figures on a board game. The leaning towers of boxes had been moved. The doorway was free of obstacles and the threshold clear. He slipped the key into the lock with a clumsy second try and they squeezed through the doorway together, hips touching. Dawn let out a girlish laugh which made Adam's heart beat a little faster. It was like a new place in there. Ben had worked hard to clear the cobwebs and detritus.

"This is amazing, isn't it?" She flicked on the hallway light illuminating the feat she'd underestimated. The old carousel had gone. He'd run the vacuum over the area rugs and shined the floor. He'd fluffed pillows and steamed the curtains. What was left was the shiny scent of lemon polish and mint upholstery spray, and fresh clean cotton left to dry in sunlight. It was an unmistakable smell.

"It's unbelievable what he got done in a few days."

"Poor Bea was at her wits end." She breezed from the sitting room to the hallway and back again. "I never noticed how nice these floors are. And this rug has got to be an antique—one of a kind." She mused, "Funny, I never really saw them," shrugging off the thought like a cardigan. "Anyway, I can't believe he finally did it."

"What a guy will do for love..." He sputtered the words, feeling stupid immediately. If she'd noticed his face had gone red, she didn't let on. Instead she marveled at the intricate bevels of the crown molding she'd never noticed before and craned her neck to admire the pictures on the wall.

"I love this picture of David." She pointed at a picture of a smiling boy, probably about fourteen at the time of the picture and just before the world for him had become too heavy. He hoisted a trophy with a test tube on the top, his grin as wide as the sky. Adam didn't intend to lean so close, but to see the picture well he stood next to Dawn so that their shoulders pressed.

"He was a good kid."

"Look at Ben," she said with as much delight as surprise. "He's something else."

"Mr. Strings," he smiled.

The Ben of old wore a slim-cut suit and a half-cocked fedora. His tie burned brightly even in black and white and popped against the grain of the gritty night club. The fancy hanky in his jacket pocket matched exactly.

"So smooth," she admired. She crossed in front of him so the rose petals tickled the side of his face. He could smell the sun in her hair and her skin was warm from the night even through the coolness of his shirt.

"That's our Ben."

He backed away suddenly, as if he'd forgotten something. He strode to the kitchen with purpose and opened the door to the garage which had been organized to look like a neat Santa's workshop, minus a box or two. Everything was in place.

"So, where are these things?" she called to him. "Are they out there?"

Adam entered sheepishly, unable to achieve the same smoothness that the man in the pictures could pull off with ease.

"I don't think they're here."

An almost imperceptible pop outside served as a tiny exclamation point. Others followed shortly, like a chorus. When he reached her back in the front room it already sounded as if a giant popcorn maker was at work in the center of Twin Oaks.

He smiled. "Okay, I know they're not here."

She tilted her head, amused and perplexed, twisting one strand of her wavy hair. "Then why are we here?"

This was the moment he both loved and hated, the single moment that could portend promise or disappointment. But there was no hiding here, no boxes to duck behind. It was all out in the open now. He could be a hero and step into the labyrinth, or he could back away and pretend that it was all a mistake.

The little pops became loud booms, and she smiled, taken off-guard. "Wow! That is some fiesta we're missing," she said. "But I don't understand why Ben would..."

He took a step toward her hoping his reddening cheeks wouldn't make him look like a scared boy. "I think he was trying to get us here alone." He rubbed a hand over his head looking at the wall of pictures that were never there before. They watched like a hopeful audience.

"What is he up to?" Now her cheeks flushed with the same deep bloom of crimson. "That's silly." She repeated it like a final blow, and her eyes drifted to the floor and out the window, taking his hopes with them. But then she spoke again, with doubt and distraction, and her eyes returned to him. "Isn't it?"

The fist in Adam's throat threw a punch to his confidence but he choked it down like a hero and spoke with certainty. "No, not really." He was as brazen as the sporadic test fires that peppered the silence like musket fire, reaching his hands out to rest on her shoulders. He traced her arms down to her hands and held them in his own. "I really like you." He'd envisioned her as his goddess in the heavens, dragging the sun across the sky, and he'd given her a line he'd used when he was in seventh grade. But this time it wasn't a line. "I don't know how to say this, but there's something here. Something real. Don't you feel it too?"

His fingers sent icy rivulets down to her core. She shivered where he couldn't see, where skin met bone.

Her voice was shaky, like a patient coming back from anesthesia, and the room looked sleepy and disconcerting. But it all made sense when she looked at him. "I like you too."

In his deep blue eyes she saw not the folly of everyday but the madness of which life was made. And before her head could understand what she was doing, she'd stood on tiptoes and leaned in to him so far that her balance had given way. She fell into him with all she had and he accepted her then and there, as if he'd been waiting forever in a world without time.

There had been kisses, yes, but none that shocked him at his depths and pulled him into the cosmos where he could barely breathe. He had to remind his heart to beat, his hands to feel, and his limbs to move, because when he felt her he was transfixed.

Then, as quickly as they'd come together, she retreated like a lost thought, crossing the room like a ghost. She didn't even look back.

He felt like a fool again, standing palms to the air, as if she were still holding him.

Dawn gave the tiniest sigh. "This is more like it." She flicked the switch on the wall and the room went so dark that he knew she was there only by her scent and by the scant light reflected in her eyes. The twin mirrors came quickly, stealthy in the dark, and she was stronger than he'd imagined.

He lay back on the fancy triple-weave rug, the one with the intricate star inlay and the burning sun. Dawn followed. He couldn't see what she'd done but he heard the fabric drop as her footsteps came close. The floorboards were cool against is legs, but her skin was warm. In perfect time with the explosions outside, her breaths came in heavy rushes. He was floating in a world he couldn't see, moving at light speed in the void. In bursts of light at her back he could see her silhouette against the night sky, skin glistening. She pulled him in like gravity and she lifted him to the heavens where they met in a world of blackness. In her eyes he could see infinity and didn't want to know anything else. There was nothing more than right now.

Mrs. Ringhaus couldn't remember a time she was as happy as Dawn. And she stayed with him through the booming and light that hammered outside. They clung together until it all when quiet and the outside world had faded.

PIGGY'S BIG ADVENTURE

The Pollack children walked softly through the grass, though the chance of being seen was close to nil. Jack had spent the rest of the night cleaning up the remains of Wilma's big party, including the host herself. The fireworks had been extravagant, loud, and at times mesmerizing, especially to the youngest, but Alton's greatest disappointment that evening had come when he'd learned that there would be no Big One.

Twelve times larger than the average Roman candle, Alton had read that it had a range of over a quarter mile, and a two hundred and twenty-five decibel boom. The Big One was more like a cannon, but last night, when Mrs. Womack had exploded, the show was cut short.

But then from the ashes of a restless sleep an idea was born in the boy that was nothing short of genius. They'd crept out before sunrise like thieves to put the steps in place. Mollie oiled the wheels of the green plastic wagon so they rolled in complete silence. Piggy sat as a lookout while Mollie towed stealthily. Alton played scout while walking a few houses ahead so he could look into side yards for forgotten treasures. Bulk trash day was coming, and rather than place eyesores at the curb as other neighborhoods did, the people of Twin Oaks stowed them away like secrets, leaning against sheds and the backsides of homes. He'd heard his mother fight for the practice until it became so. So he knew where to look for the discarded components of his greatest project yet.

"Here!" he called, looking to the ground where a deep curb met a tuft of grass. It gleamed like silver. "I knew it was somewhere around here." Pigg leapt from the deep pocket of the wagon and extricated the shining remains of what was once Mrs. Ringhaus's bra. But the children didn't know anything of cup support or moisture wicking materials. They saw something else.

"Yes!" Mollie clapped cheerfully. "This is just what we need." She piled what turned out to be several pieces of wispy feeling clothing into a heap.

The treasure hunt continued past the newlyweds' house where they clipped a stack of scrap papers and three sticks of glue. Then onward to Mr. Chalmers', whose house had always been like a holy grail to Alton, filled with rarities he would never see. But he gasped wildly when he saw the oversized box in a remote corner of the back yard. The entire contents were tucked inside the wagon, Pigg sacrificing his seat for the cause.

"Tongs, crockpot. Look at the size of this rope!" Alton whispered greedily as if it were Christmas.

But there was one thing left to acquire before they could get started, and he knew where to find it, at least when it wasn't in his father's pocket. It would be hard to slip into the shed unnoticed, but it turned out that he didn't need to enter. He found what he was looking for on a patch of dewy grass.

Each yard supported Pigg's dream, contributing its own perfume. Mrs. Macmillan's leant the subtle hint of roses; Mrs. Granger's, always cinnamon. Their own yard was a harder to discern. It was a complex bouquet, bitter and sweet.

"We'll set up here." Alton consulted a piece of construction paper marked with white crayon, a true blueprint, and ticked off steps as they were met to his satisfaction. "No, no. The tape goes on the other end. Hold that piece and then twist it. There you go. Yes, draw a stripe with the marker. Good. We're going to have to wait for this to dry before we can think about using it."

He laid pieces together like a puzzle waiting to be assembled, putting the priority piece in a swatch of dry grass where it would become useful later.

Mollie took the orders and consulted her own sketch. It was marked with flower stamps and loopy handwriting she'd been working on all year. She grabbed Pigg and turned the little one around, wrapping a long light swatch of fabric in the opposite direction.

"There," She said, satisfied. "That's a cape."

She reached into the satchel she wore at her hip and pulled out a pair of familiar albeit enormous mirrored sunglasses that sparkled over Pigg's eyes as if they'd been forged with real gold.

"Perfect!"

She picked out the last contribution from Mrs. Ringhaus's pile, securing the strap under Pigg's chin, so the two round pieces flanked the child's head like mouse ears.

"And your helmet," she asked as she bent eye to goggle, "does that feel all right, Piggy?"

The chubby child nodded with such emphasis that both the eye and headwear flipped askew. She adjusted without missing a beat and checked with the commander with a salute of their own design.

"Captain Pigg, ready for duty, sir." She whipped the back of her hand to the top of her forehead and brought it down with a twirl. The smallest one stood with a puffed out chest and a million-dollar smile.

Alton was satisfied but busy with his own tinkering.

The big pot was the perfect size to serve as a platform. Pigg could stand on top of it without any risk of it toppling over or tipping to one side. He measured the distance between himself and this new platform with a pair of barbecue tongs rescued from Mr. Chalmers' bulk trash. Everything was almost ready. He extracted a long rope from the green plastic wagon and inspected the part he had laid out to dry. The quick wave and flap of his hands was the signal that they were ready to go. All three children had obviously practiced because they moved stealthily at once and in unison.

Mollie picked up the smaller child, helping with the step up into the wagon. Alton flipped over the pot and loaded the long rope and tongs inside, grabbing lastly the piece he was confident had dried.

He motioned to Mrs. Womack's yard with one finger over his mouth. The woman was up and around now that the sun had surfaced. She and Gustav milled around the outskirts of her front lawn pulling up everything from discarded slips of paper to weeds. They were studying the woman's patterns, waiting for her to stop and hold her head as she had every ten feet or so. And when she did, they snuck into her back yard without a peep from the woman or her dog, genius or not.

They saw what their father had cleaned, and not cleaned, as last night had unfolded. After the fireworks, simple cleaning was put aside for the more pressing issue that Mrs. Womack had brought up in the form of expelled alcohol and apologetic exclamations. They knew that the glitter was still on the far table. Mollie grabbed some and sprinkled it on the paper craft she'd started, finishing her cone with a thick coating of sparkling silver.

"Here!" Alton called, victoriously, eyes glowing with joy.

"It's huge," Mollie stated the obvious, a habit that had made Alton cringe most of the time. But this morning it only fueled his delight.

"I know." He smiled. "Put the cone on."

She did so dutifully, another salute following each step. She pulled three curved pieces of painted cardboard from her satchel and secured them at the base. Then she pulled out a much larger pair, painted bright red like the others. But she attached these so that they stuck straight out and flat, fattest end to thinnest, and saluted one last time.

Alton inspected what they'd done and compared it to the notes on his page. "Okay, we're ready."

He called Piggy over, and as always the youngest child gave a fervent and immediate response. The glasses tottered and the bra wobbled, but still the youngest offered a chubby-handed salute while stepping up onto the overturned crockpot.

"I'm going to need a hand with this, Mollie," he instructed, and his sister did something that wasn't in the plan. She hesitated.

Alton was too excited to become annoyed. The sun would be too bright for them to hide soon, and that Womack woman was getting her wits back by the second. He could hear her talking to the dog.

"Alton, are you sure about this? It is really big." She squinted hard, as if it hurt to imagine.

He sighed, irritation brewing. "Of course I'm sure." He took a deep breath to clear any bother from his voice. And then he smiled, as the adults did when they said *let's go do something fun,* and it was really a trip to the dentist. "You ready, Pigg?"

The small child gave a nod, and with Mollie's help Alton lifted the big project onto the pot platform just behind the goggle-clad captain. He wrapped the long rope around his baby sibling and around the Big One, outfitted with nose cone, fins, and two giant wings. He then crossed the yard to the dry patch of grass and grabbed the most important component to the master plan. It had been the most difficult to imagine procuring, and ended up being the easiest part to find. Jack had left an entire book of them discarded right outside the shed.

Alton gripped the tongs hard in one hand making sure not to drop what he held. He flicked against his other hand until the sandpaper sound made a tiny pop and the faint scent of sulfur cut through the whitewashed smell of morning. The match ignited on the first strike and he leaned in quickly to the little one waiting bravely on the pot. The rocket fuse had been lit, and Piggy's countdown had begun.

DAPHNE'S GIFT

*H*e'd come home with a gift that morning: a camera, how fitting. She'd cupped the lens in her hand and looked through the viewfinder from the bathroom window into the sunny world of Twin Oaks. She'd sat there all day, clicking images of the neighborhood from the only place in the house where she could see everything. The loop stretched out in front of her, like child's model, and she'd forgotten how good it felt to be behind everything for once.

In another life that was how she saw him, always looking in from the other side. She watched Echo through her lens. He surfed and skated, scuba dove and jumped from planes; and there was Daphne, safely stowed-away from the action, clicking away like a cicada, as he smiled and laughed for the camera. She wasn't unhappy. It wasn't a hard life then, being rich kids, the only worry being which adventure to engage in next.

So when he brought the new camera, she wasn't surprised. They both knew by now how hard it was to surprise her. Sometimes ideas came to her in a flash, tiny snippets of events set in tableau, like images set in watercolor or chiaroscuro. More often than not they gave a vague impression of what was to come. Other times it was something that had already happened, reminding through Daphne that it should not be forgotten. Once, when she was a young girl, she'd picked up a hand mirror on her mother's vanity, and in the reflection she'd seen the woman much younger in an embrace with a man that wasn't Daphne's father.

Even then she knew it was something never to speak of. Just like she knew that the smell of metal and blood drifted in and out of her dreams. Echo had had his doubts, and he soothed and assured himself as he pressed on with the grand plan. On the starting line, back in her track days, she was like a statue. She'd wait patiently in the blocks, starting on a dime at the sound of the gun. Echo had always jumped the gun. That was his way.

Now the two of them were here in this round little place. The city was far away, and it was all supposed to be good for her, for her troubles, or so they'd said. In truth, they didn't know real trouble from ice cream. It was she that *knew things*.

She had known that Echo would be bringing something for her, not from premonition but because she knew that today would be about presents. The ladies had brought one when they arrived, a welcome wrapped in pretty bows, as if it were someone's birthday. So why shouldn't he bring her a present? There was nothing spooky about it. She'd simply expected it.

In the bathroom it smelled like spring flowers, and the light glinted off fixtures she'd found so appealing at that first open house. It darted from the window to the sink then off the sliver handles onto the claw foot tub, to the remarkable surprise she'd received from the ladies' association. It stayed, focused and magnified, then radiating from the blade, sleek and polished to a magnificent shine. She could see herself reflected in the sliver, no distortion to blur her vision.

She toyed with it, poised the dagger on her fingers admiring the bejeweled handle. It could be mother of pearl, but she imagined that it felt like an ancient bone. Bloody rubies and weeping sapphires and emeralds that gleamed like serpent's eyes played in the darting light that danced off the blade. The weight of it pushed against her hands as if it belonged, carving out a groove in her flesh. She could feel it, as if it were at once heavy and weightless. It was so easy to handle, yet at the same time too much for her. It was strange how readily that changed from second to second.

She liked it in here, the silence punctuated by the clicks of her finger on the shutter. The camera was cold when rested against her pale cheek. She vacillated between Echo's gift and the blade. It was so hard to choose.

The neighborhood looked so clean in the morning, uncluttered and full of promise. She loved the way the squirrels held court over toppled garbage cans, and the way that the ladybugs crowded on windowpanes like gossiping mothers. They were respectful, not like others who grunted like beasts and shouted in vulgar tones at the first sign of a social gathering. The garish lights and steaming pig meat had made her feel sick. Not to mention that gross display later. She hadn't caught it in person but had taken enough shots to recreate the incident in stop-motion if she chose. She flipped through the images in rapid succession, eyes wide as that screaming woman dropped her shorts. It was mesmerizing, the way her face contorted in pain and joy. It was at once captivating and freeing too, and so much better without sound.

It had been too much for her, even for the brief time she spent in that woman's yard. She was disgusted with the party, yes. But it was better than staying home with the nightmares. They came now even when she was awake. She could see the blood on the floor in the living room, peeking out from underneath the fancy carpeting. It followed her even here to her sparkling bathroom, even when she shook her head violently to repel it.

She'd had a bad feeling that something was going to happen, which was why Echo should never have left. But that was not his way. He shrugged off her dreams and worries, always looking toward the best, even when he knew in his heart she'd never been wrong. He had a way of picking and choosing what he'd believe. She knew before the sickness came that there was a life inside her, just as she'd known that the baby would never have a chance. He was such an optimist. But she never had a choice.

Only the ladies knew; she'd told them things she didn't dare tell anyone, not Echo or the doctor. As they sat sipping her lips slipped open like flood gates bringing the tears with them, and she'd told them about her dreams and about the blood, and how it never went away. Abigail had held her hand and the emptiness faded with each warm sip of special tea. She found herself laughing and smiling with them, sharing her deepest secrets and dreams.

Annabelle sat at her other side. She had falsely assumed that the one in red had liked her the least. But she sat stroking her hair lightly and speaking gently in Daphne's ear. It felt good to be wrong. She found herself explaining that sometimes she sank so low that it felt as if there was no air, only a long, hollow tunnel crushing her from the outside in. And then on other days the world seemed to hurtle so quickly past her that it felt like she was travelling at light speed, and it was hard to grasp a single experience. How unsure she felt, and it got so much worse when the baby was gone.

"I feel like a piece of me is missing."

Annabelle looked at Abigail and in turn to the quiet one in blue before responding in earnest.

"We can help you with that."

Annabelle touched her hand and Daphne couldn't shake the feeling that she'd never feel alone again.

"We want you to join us now." The ladies leaned in on either side in a shoulder to shoulder embrace. Only Agnes sat it out. She looked out the window watching the neighbor's day unfold. Abigail reached into her burlap bag and pulled out a wrapped bundle of dried herbs and sticks, fragrant with spice and earth, vaguely sugary like her extraordinary tea.

"At night, for your nightmares. They won't haunt you anymore."

She'd clutched the bundle in both hands when Annabelle stopped her from moving any further. She pulled the gift from her own bag, wrapped in ribbons twisted in intricate curls. She pulled them one by one, the reds and blues with the yellows, and lastly the green. Abigail leaned in close, giving a little gasp when the dagger was in sight. And Annabelle rose beside her closing her hands over the gift and speaking gently.

She toyed with it now, flipping the dagger from one hand to the other, then giving it a rest to take a look through her new camera. Echo loved her, which she didn't doubt. But he could never understand the depths and heights of her fear and despair. He couldn't help that he was always hoping, as silly as it seemed.

The Pollack children appeared in the view finder, the youngest centered in its crosshairs, wobbling across Mrs. Womack's lawn in the most peculiar dress. The big one looked like a mad scientist from a black and white thriller. The girl wielded a measuring tape like a lasso, cutting swaths of imaginary fabric in the air. But the baby? She couldn't make out what the little one was doing or what the tyke wore. But they were doing a much better job picking up the pieces of the party than the woman in the other yard, and they were smiling so freely. It was genuine joy. Before she could snap a picture, they'd disappeared into the fat woman's yard and out of range.

She surfaced like an obscene pat of butter, slowly oozing her way onto blades of grass like they were cooked greens. She didn't see the children or the wagon, or anything important for that matter. She kept stooping down, curling over at the center of her lawn, that dog pacing beside her like a detective. He kept looking at the gate as if alerted to the intruders' presence, clearly the brains behind the operation. And no doubt, the best part of the view. Womack was pale and unwieldy, squinting into the sun that was not yet too bright. So dramatic, so foolish this woman, this insignificant speck in the scheme of things. It wasn't hard to imagine the neighborhood without her.

You just need to do us this one favor...

She clutched the ladies' dagger like a good luck charm, rubbing her finger over the pink stone in the handle.

Her back was to Daphne now, head ducked so far down that it was hard to tell the woman from the pig in her gaudy decorations. She was talking lightly to that dog, as if he was talking back, and he grinned like he owned the world. Yet he kept looking toward that back fence. The window opened without a sound. She sat on the sill, camera in hand, her good luck charm balanced on her knees. If she craned her neck, she got a better view of Mrs. Womack picking up scraps of paper, and of the dog that wouldn't leave her side.

He sniffed the air and licked at that woman's legs, but she was preoccupied with the remains of a piñata. Had she any brains she would have seen the dog was agitated. Did he know something was about to happen? He paced from the woman to the edge of the grass, expecting to lead her from her spot, until frustrated he darted away on his own.

The children were playing on the other side of her white picket fence. The little one stood on a platform tied to something she couldn't make out. Children were so strange with their world of pretend. They never know what danger lurks ahead, what pain they will soon find. The girl seemed to be chanting something; the boy smiled wildly. And Mrs. Womack stood not ten feet away, none the wiser to anything that was about to unfold, or the fact that she was all alone.

Soon the loop would be bustling with newspaper boys, and trash collectors, runners and mailmen. It would be crawling with activity, so many people to see.

Daphne jumped from the window leaving the camera. She moved swiftly past the sleepy houses, running until her legs burned like hellfire. She held the dagger aloft, clutching it like it had become part of her, and straight for Mrs. Womack. She only hoped to get there in time.

ASHES

Daphne had run hurdles at a fancy prep school where navy blue stripes sliced girls in bright white uniforms clean in half. She seemed to give off an ultraviolet light when she ran so quickly that she'd almost forgotten to breathe. Why memories of high school had surfaced as she sped past neighborhood houses was beyond her, but the world was hard to grasp as she moved in what seemed like slow motion.

She'd flown from the house like a ghost, dagger gripped tightly in her hand with one target in sight. She needed to get to that woman, and quickly. The need burned in her throat but there was no time for tears. The sun was almost up, and by the time it lit the sky it would be too late.

She was upon Mrs. Womack in seconds, hair plastered to the side of her face in cold sweat that was more nerves than exertion. The woman gasped at the sight of her, eyes wide like a cow's before the slaughter. The dagger came plunging down, and in one panicked exhale Daphne found her calm, like light at the end of an airless tunnel. It came in a cool, emotionless voice.

"Where is the gate?"

"The what?"

"The gate!" Her voice never deviated, but she'd closed whatever gap was between them, raising the dagger even higher over her shoulder. The fevered woman's eyes darted quickly behind Daphne to a concealed latch within the fence hidden behind a spring loaded square, and before she regained the capacity to make words her young neighbor had disappeared.

The sizzling was the first thing she noticed, as loud and as clear as it had been in the Wile E. Coyote cartoons, the exaggerated fried egg sound of a decidedly lit fuse. Then the smell of sulfur and blown-out candles. It hit her like a wave of nausea, catching in her nostrils and the back of her throat and stayed in the strands of her hair.

And when she saw Pigg standing there like Joan of Arc on a crockpot, she lunged at the makeshift platform like a long jumper hoping to knock the baby loose. But this time she'd fallen short.

The fuse glowed like a cherry despite her best effort to dim it with spit, fingers and breath. The child didn't squirm or ask for help. Little Piggy looked frozen, a statue waiting for immortality.

The other children's voices came in and out of her consciousness as she drew the knife down and across the ropes. She carved across them like a demented cellist keeping heated rhythm over the same groove. One length gone. Then two loops fell. Almost there when the taste of sweat stung her lips and eyes. She could smell the no-tears shampoo, the grass, and then the fire before the whole world exploded.

Then came the feeling of dripping wet, clinging to her favorite t-shirt stained red, and the O peeking out from a background gone crimson and a scent that had haunted her, like the familiar sound of a mother ripped with torment.

"Not my booooo-oooy!"

April Pollack burst into the yard just as her baby was blown across Mrs. Womack's yard with the Big One on his back. She was beautiful even then in her white silk nightgown, even as she screamed, her neat hair gone wayward as she ripped it out in clumps.

Mrs. Womack looked as though she was about to drop dead, running as quickly as she could to the Pollack's, pounding on the door like a madwoman. Jack had come first, emerging from his shed with a bucket full of water and an apron around his waist. He bolted across the yard, lifting Pigg, whose charred black body lay limp in his arms. He brought the child to his mother, who wept freely in the morning air, wiping at cheeks with panicked hands and trying to make the wet spots disappear.

He handed Piggy off to April without a word and doubled back into the streamer strewn yard to search for what was left of his baby boy's foot.

April stared at the baby whose lashes had fluttered like a suffering bird's wings, closed then open, once and for all focused on his mother's face. She looked into his eyes and spoke to him as if they were the only people there, like they were back in the pale green room decorated with lambs and lions. She used the soft voice that only he and Solomon knew, the one his older siblings had already forgotten.

"Piggy, my sweet Piggy. No other child like you could be mine. No other mother in the world could be yours. No one could love a soul the way I love my sweet Piggy..."

Mrs. Granger had emerged through the gates like an apparition, grey khaki slacks and jacket, fine dusky shirt in matching silk. The woman looked as if she'd prepared for hours for this, but then Mrs. Granger was always ready for anything, a habit of hers to look good no matter what the hour or event. She stood close to April, whose hair stuck up in the places where she'd yanked and pulled it to shreds.

Her eyes, bleary with tears, wore the mark of her own heartbreak. The older woman stood tall over her, and leaned in like a shady tree, under which both April and Piggy found shelter. There in that shadow she stroked the boy, pulled her hair back into place, and feeling Mrs. Granger behind her, straightened up as if nothing was wrong.

Meanwhile Jack ransacked the yard. He bolted spot to spot like a boxing kangaroo, digging up pieces of confetti, tossing aside discarded maracas, hoping for the best of finds and fearing for the worst. The ambulance echoed through the cool morning, sirens rising up like steam off the dewy grass. He felt Wilma come up beside him—bless that woman for her heart. She was red faced and crying when she told him, as if it were somehow her fault, what had happened to his baby. She was about to speak when Gustav bounded frantically over a mound of errant grass and a loose clot of dirt.

"Here Jack," she called. "Just Jack, this way!" She waved frantically, brushing soil from her golden boy's find. She waved the find triumphantly at the man who sprinted her way, and back in the opposite direction once he had the foot in hand. He spoke briefly with the paramedics who surveyed the scene, as perplexed as aliens who might have crash landed on a routine tour of Twin Oaks.

Mrs. Granger walked with April, who now looked much more like herself now that she'd borrowed a jacket from her stately friend. Her shoulders felt stronger under the president's able arm. The tears disappeared as if they were never there. The two spoke in a mixture of whispers and facial gestures, and when she reached Jack, she handed the child off as if he were a bag of soil for the back yard, then backed away with her friend to a safe distance. The paramedics worked on Piggy, who was neither panicked nor calm but aware. The child looked around the crowded yard as if seeing the world for the first time.

Dawn had heard the ambulance and panicked; Adam's

fingers, still entwined with hers, were nearly yanked from the sockets when she bolted upright and ran for the door. It wasn't often that she slept with young computer tycoons on her neighbors' floor, so when she'd stepped over the threshold, forgetting for the moment that she was still nude, Adam was there to hand her the sundress he'd admired so much the previous evening. If there wasn't a crisis at hand, she might have felt wicked or ashamed, but Adam squeezed her shoulders tightly as they moved swiftly passed the surrounding houses, until that glorious moment when she saw that her girls were okay.

Mr. and Mrs. Chalmers had come from Dawn's house, with two the two girls in tow. They took to Piggy's siblings like lifelong friends, the older girl putting a hand on Alton's shoulder. Piggy had never seen his older brother cry. Mollie stared off into space, not looking for rockets but escape, and Lucy seemed to respect that, joining her in the silent watching like they could somehow find it together. Gustav, curled up between them, and when the little girls started smiling, he felt like a king.

Ben, who was the smoothest guy Adam knew, spoke to the young man who alternated between shaking uncontrollably and standing stock still. "Hey Alton, I've got a stack of *Scientific Monthly* with your name on them."

Adam felt like the world had been lifted from his shoulders. He would have felt guilty had it not been for Dawn, who rested her head on his shoulder and held his hand firmly between her fingers long after they'd walked into Wilma's yard. The girls had blushed and hugged him tightly before scurrying away from the turmoil. It was Becca who looked over her shoulder with a wink when they were safely out of sight.

He watched until Dawn's door shut behind them, locking them safely away from what was ahead. And when he turned back he had to question what that might be. She walked behind him, pushing slowly. The wheels needed to be oiled or adjusted. He wouldn't know without looking, but he could hear the squeaks and see the man under the blanket, bent up like a small child.

He ran to them before they hit the scene.

"Mom, what are you doing?"

Agnes wore a simple t-shirt and a pair of clean cotton shorts, as she had when she was younger and they'd played at the beach. She talked as if she were instructing kindergarten, never taking her eyes off Adam's father, who looked somehow different today.

"I thought I'd take the boss here for a walk. It's as good a day as any." She took a deep breath and waited, as if it were a question awaiting the man in the chair's approval. He smiled weakly and she placed her hand in his. He wrapped his fingers around hers giving an obvious, albeit weak squeeze.

She mouthed to Adam with hope in her eyes, "*Better, right?*"

He did look better than he had in a while. He thought the stress had altered his eyes.

"*Where's Hettie?*" he mouthed back.

"I gave her the day off." And then Agnes continued out loud for the benefit of anyone who was in earshot, "I'm going to be spending a lot more time at home. With my family."

He was so intent on the revelation that he didn't hear her behind him or brace for the arms around his waist. Dawn held him tightly, as if she needed him there, and kissed him boldly for all the world to see.

Agnes didn't sway or swoon. She didn't look toward the ladies who hovered together on the tragic lawn like specters in embrace. She smiled, matching the blush that spread across Adam's cheeks with her own.

"Son, I'm glad you're finally happy." She kissed the man in the chair on the top of his head before rolling him as far from Mrs. Womack's yard as they could get.

Even when Echo held Daphne tightly in the warm fleece blanket, she shivered in his arms.

"I don't want this," her voice trembled as she dropped the dagger to the ground.

"Where did you get that ?" His question fell away as his eyes drifted to the woman heading toward them.

"Nice save, honey." Her voice was unaffected and even despite the ambulance that blocked half the street and the blood spattered party decorations littering the grass. She plucked up the dagger like a discarded toy and leaned into Annabelle as if sharing a dirty joke. Echo's body tensed.

"Would you look at who's all hot and bothered?" She pitched toward him so that no mystery lay between them and lowered her voice. "You look tired; haven't you been sleeping?"

Daphne's voice came ragged and strong: "Bitch!"

Annabelle let out a hearty laugh, "My, you have such spirit." She used the dagger like a toy, tracing down the line of her neck to her collarbone, and lower. "I'm just playing. That's just how we are." She purred. "It's not for everyone, though. Shame that it's not for you." She pointed at the young woman with the golden knife when a bell like voice cleaved the air.

"Leave her alone, Annabelle."

Abigail came up from Daphne's other side, smoothing her hair. "Don't pay her any attention." She scowled at Annabelle, who backed away like a threatened snake, and added with equal venom, "Some of us just aren't cut out for this." She winked at Echo before ambling down the grass toward the two ladies who embraced on Mrs. Womack's lawn. "We'll see you around."

"You okay?" Abigail's attention turned to her one friend, and Daphne's voice was even and sure.

She said with uncharacteristic certainty, "Yes, I think I am." She was indeed fine, or at least she was going to be fine, despite the morning's chaos. Echo was a good man, whose tears came now in spurts of relief, tempered by sighs of joy. And she loved him for both.

"Abigail, you've got something right there..." She

swiped at her friend's forehead, aware that for the first time she'd made note of the smallest detail occurring not before or after, but right now.

"Where?"

"Right there!" She poked a finger under the brilliant paisley bandana that covered Abigail's head, pulling out what she thought was a piece of fuzz or pollen.

"Oh this! This is just my hair!" She giggled girlishly, pulling at the strands of white hair until she could twirl them around her finger. "Isn't it beautiful?"

April felt much better now with Mrs. Granger's arms around her. What started as one around her shoulder had now wrapped her like a snake, and with each squeeze she could feel the paralyzing fear drop away.

"Please, April," she spoke into her ear. "Why don't you come over for tea?"

The words were dreams in her ears, and filled her head so that there was nothing else.

"Right now?" she asked, sleepy. All the tightness and tension had disappeared.

"Right now," the president cooed. "I need you right now."

April felt the spiraling madness circle around her as Mrs. Granger loosened her hold. It was wild in this yard, this horrible morning when the world had spun out of her grasp.

"There's something I've been dying to show you."

April felt herself moving toward the ambulance and kissing her small child goodbye before setting off with Mrs. Granger to the house she'd never seen from the inside. "That would make me happy."

Mrs. Womack wrung her hands and paced semicircles around the ambulance where they worked on Just Jack's little boy. If Gus were here, he'd assure her that this whole thing wasn't her fault. But she'd told Gus to help those young girls, to cheer them up because they were so frightened. So she stood behind the ambulance watching like a stranger as the doctor tried to put that poor child back together. The blood pressure machine beeped and the intravenous was set and soon they'd ship him off to the hospital and it would all be okay. Gussie would tell her that. She was sure he would if he had he been at her side.

But he wasn't there. And she was sure Just Jack hated her, hated her like poison, for the firecrackers, and the thrown-up tequila.

She didn't see him pop out of the ambulance. "They're getting his vitals and cleaning up the wounds. Now that they've got it on ice..." he couldn't bear to say what it was, "I think it's going to be okay." He stood so close that his tattooed arm touched her bare shoulder, and when he pulled away self-consciously, he brought her self-consciousness with him.

"I'm so sorry," she said, intending not to blubber, intending to be strong. But her words flowed in a torrent of grief and regret. Her eyes twinkled with all the emotion that tied joy to sadness, all the admiration and woe, all the terrible beauty of disaster wrapped in unforgiving love.

Jack didn't give a damn if anyone saw, and he took Wilma in his arms and kissed her hard and long, for all the longing and hardship they'd both encountered and endured. And she opened herself to him in a rush of yearning that made clear to him that it was her that he'd wanted all along.

He leaned into the back of the ambulance, which was now ready to pull away, and reached one hand down to the woman who'd always waited. "I want you with me." He lifted her up, holding her close as they rode away together, shutting out the view behind them.

From a wooden bench not so far away, Mrs. MacMillan looked on, holding her husband's bony hand, as they waved goodbye.

Made in the USA
Lexington, KY
01 February 2015